P9-BYU-486

The Devil You Know

MAR 2016

Also by K. J. Parker

THE DEVIL YOU KNOW

K. J. PARKER

A TOM DOHERTY ASSOCIATES BOOK
NEW YORK

This is a work of fiction. All of the characters, organizations, and events portrayed in this novella are either products of the author's imagination or are used fictitiously.

THE DEVIL YOU KNOW

Copyright © 2016 by Tom Holt

Cover art by Jon Foster
Cover designed by Christine Foltzer

Edited by Jonathan Strahan

All rights reserved.

A Tor.com Book
Published by Tom Doherty Associates
175 Fifth Avenue
New York, NY 10010

www.tor.com

Tor® is a registered trademark of Tom Doherty Associates, LLC.

ISBN 978-0-7653-8447-8 (ebook)
ISBN 978-0-7653-8789-9 (trade paperback)

First Edition: March 2016

The Devil You Know

I DON'T DO EVIL when I'm not on duty, just as prostitutes tend not to have sex on their days off. My ideal off-shift day starts with a hot bath and the scent of black tea, followed by an hour on my balcony with a good book; then a stroll through the busy streets to view an art exhibition, hear a sermon or a philosophical debate, or simply admire the mosaics in the Blue Temple; lunch on the terrace beside the river with a friend or two (not work colleagues); an afternoon with no plans or commitments, so I can be totally spontaneous; a light supper; then to the theatre or the opera, and so to bed.

A really bad off-shift day starts before sunrise, with an urgent message to say that something's come up, it's so delicate and important that the other shift can't handle it, and I'm to report to some hick town thirty miles away, dressed, shaved, and ready for business in twenty minutes. You may argue that I get days like that because I'm so good at what I do, better than anyone else in the department, so really it's the nearest our organisation can get to a pat on the back and a well-done. Maybe. It doesn't make it any less annoying when it happens.

You don't have to enjoy your work to be good at it. Frankly, I don't like what I do. It offends me. But I'm the best in the business.

~

"Quite a catch," the briefing officer told me. "We need more intellectuals."

That was news to me. "Do we? Why?"

"To maintain the balance. And to demonstrate the perils of intellectual curiosity taken to excess."

"Is that possible?" I asked, but he just grinned.

"That's the line to take," he said. "And you say it like you mean it. I guess that's what makes you such a star."

Of course, I have no input into policy. "From what the brief says he doesn't need any persuading," I said. "Do you really need me for this? Surely it's just a case of witnessing a signature and writing out a receipt."

"You were asked for. Specifically. By name."

I frowned. "By Divisional Command?"

"By the customer."

I don't like it when they call them that. "Are you sure?"

"By name," he repeated. "A well-informed man, evidently."

"Nobody's heard of me."

"He has."

I changed my mind about the assignment. I've remained obscure and pseudonymous all this time for a reason. "And he's all ready to sign?"

"We didn't approach him. He came to us."

Oh dear. "Has it occurred to you," I said, "that the whole thing could be a setup? A trick? Entrapment?"

He smiled. "Yes," he said. "Take care, now. Have a nice day."

⁓

Oh dear cubed.

Entrapment is not unknown in my line of work. As witness Fortunatus of Perimadeia, a great sage who was active about four hundred years ago. Fortunatus conjured a demon, trapped him in a bottle, and distilled him into raw energy. Likewise the stories about Tertullian, who challenged the Prince of Darkness to a logic contest and won. Both apocryphal, needless to say, but stories like that give people ideas. What more prestigious scalp to nail to your tent-post, after all, than one of us?

I read the brief again. I insist on having one, written on real parchment with real ink; physical, material. It's regarded as an eccentricity, but because of my outstanding record I'm allowed to have them. I find that reading words with mortal eyes gets me into the right mind-set for dealing with human beings. Attention to detail, you see. Proverbially I'm in it, so why not?

~

The appointment wasn't till two o'clock, which gave me the morning. I decided to make the most of it. I walked up the Catiline Way to see the spring flowers in the Victory Gardens, then spent a delightful hour or so at the Emilian House, where a very promising young artist sponsored by the duchess had put on a show; stand-alone icons, diptychs and triptychs, very classical but with an elusive hint of originality; above all, genuine feeling, such as only comes through genuine faith. The artist was there, a shy, unassuming young man with long, dark hair woven into knots. I commissioned an icon from him for forty nomismata—the Invincible Sun and military saints standing facing, holding labarum and globus cruciger. The poor boy looked stunned when I suggested the price, but then it's the duty of those who are in a position to do so to support the fine arts.

I still had an hour to kill, so I wandered down into the Tanner's Quarter, sharp left at the Buttermarket cross into Bookbinders' Street; nosed around the booksellers' stalls, picked up a few early editions. "You wouldn't happen to have," I asked, "the latest Saloninus?"

The man looked at me. "What do you mean, latest? He hasn't written anything for years."

"Ah. What's his most recent?"

The man shrugged. "Probably the *Institutes*. I haven't got that one," he added. "We don't get much call for that sort of thing." He looked at me, making a professional assessment. "I've got a very nice late edition of the *Perfumed Garden of Experience*."

"With pictures?"

"Of course with pictures."

I didn't ask the price. A book of no interest whatsoever to me, naturally, except in a broad professional sense; but the late editions are very rare, and the quality of the artwork is actually very good, regardless of the subject matter. Money changed hands; then I said, "So what Saloninus have you got?"

"Hold on, let's see. I've got two old *Moral Dialogues* and—oh, you'll like this. Forgot I had it. Limited numbered edition, best white vellum, illuminated capitals, the whole nine yards."

"Sounds good. Which book?"

"What? Oh, right." He squinted at the tiny letters on the brass tube. *"Beyond Good and Evil."*

"Perfect," I said. "I'll have it."

~

At two o'clock precisely by the Temple bell (it's five minutes fast, in fact, but since all the time in the Empire is officially taken from it, who gives a damn?) I turned down a narrow alley, found a small door in a brick wall, and knocked. No answer. I counted to ten, then gently rearranged the position of the wards inside the lock. "Hello," I called out, and went through into a charming little knot-garden, with diamond-shaped herb beds bordered with box and lavender. In the middle was a sundial; beside it was a handsome carved rosewood chair; in the chair was an old man, sleeping.

I stood over him and carefully nudged his brain back to consciousness. He looked up at me and blinked. "Who the hell are you?"

I smiled. "You wanted to see me."

"Oh." He frowned. "You're him, then."

"Yes."

"You're not—" He stopped. I grinned. "I expect they all say that."

"Most of them."

He stood up. It cost him some effort and pain. I eased the pain slightly; not enough to be obvious. "You might as well come inside," he said.

His study opened onto the garden. I imagine he liked to sit with the doors open, in the spring and summer. It was a stereotypical scholar's room; books and papers everywhere, walls floor-to-ceiling with bookshelves; an ornately carved oak desk with a sort of ebony throne behind it, a low three-legged stool on the other side. I got the stool, naturally. I made myself comfortable. I can do that, just by shortening a few small bones in my spine.

"First things first," I said, and pulled out the book I'd just bought. Not the *Perfumed Garden*. "Could you autograph it for me, please?"

He peered down a very long nose at it. "Oh, that," he said.

"Please?"

He sighed and flipped the lid off a plain brass inkwell. "I remember that edition," he said. "Tacky. Full of spelling mistakes. Still, they gave me thirty nomismata for it, so what the hell." He pulled it out of its tube, unrolled the first six inches, and scrawled what I assume was his signature diagonally across the top. "You shouldn't buy secondhand books, you know," he said, pushing it back across the desk at me. "You're taking the bread out of the writer's mouth. Worse than stealing."

"I'll bear that in mind," I said.

He was bald, with a huge fat tidal wave of a double chin and liver spots on the backs of his hands. Once, though, he'd have been strikingly handsome. Not a tall man, but stocky. Probably physically strong, before he went to seed. "It's an honour to meet you," I said. "Of course, I've read everything you've written."

He blinked at me, then said, "Everything?"

"Oh yes. The *Dialogues,* the *Consolation of Philosophy,* the *Critique of Pure Reason,* the *Principles of Mathematics.* And the other stuff. The forged wills, the second sets of books, the IOUs, the signed confessions—"

"Extracted," he pointed out, "under duress."

"Yes," I said, "but true nevertheless. Everything you ever wrote, every last scrap. You might be amused to hear, incidentally, that in four hundred years' time a promissory note written by you to honour a gambling debt of twelve gulden will sell at auction in Beal Bohec for eighteen thousand nomismata. The buyer will be an agent acting for the Duke of Beloisa, the foremost collector of his day." I smiled. "You never paid back the twelve gulden."

He shrugged. "Didn't I? Can't remember. And anyway, the game was rigged."

"By you. Loaded dice. Thank you for that," I said, holding up the book he'd just signed. "For what it's worth, I think it's the very best thing you've done."

"Coming from you—" He hesitated. "You are him, aren't you? About the—"

"About the contract, yes."

He looked at me as though for the first time. "You've read my books."

"Yes."

He took a deep breath. "What did you think of them? Honestly."

"Honestly?"

"You're capable of being honest?"

I sighed. "Yes, of course. And honestly, I think they're simply brilliant. You ruthlessly deconstruct conventional morality, proving it to be the garbled echoes of long-dead superstitions and tribal expedients, and call for a new, rational reevaluation of all values. You demonstrate beyond question that there is no such thing as absolute good or absolute evil. That, together with your revolutionary doctrine of sides, is probably your greatest legacy, surpassing even your seminal scientific and artistic achievements, though personally I believe your Fifth Symphony is the supreme artistic accomplishment of the human race and on its own entirely answers the question, what was Mankind *for*? So, yes, I liked them. Honestly."

He considered me for a while. "Yes, well. You would say that."

"Yes. But as it so happens, I mean it."

"Maybe." Without looking down, he reached for the horn cup on the left side of the desk. It was empty; I surreptitiously half-filled it with apple brandy, his favourite. He took a sip, didn't seem to notice anything out of the ordinary. "I set out to prove that you and your kind don't exist."

"Define my kind."

"Gods." Another sip; a slight frown. "Devils. Goblins, ghosts, elves, and sprites. But you liked my books."

"You're seeking to enter into a contractual relationship with someone you regard as a myth."

"I write stuff," he said. "I don't necessarily believe it myself."

"I do."

"Yes, well." He shrugged. "You're the public. And anyway, how can you possibly believe it? You're living proof it's wrong."

"I'm convinced by your arguments about the origins of conventional morality. Which happen, by the way, to be true."

"Are they?" He looked surprised. "Well, that's nice. Look," he said. "About the other stuff."

"Ah yes."

"It's true," he said. "I've done a lot of bad things."

"Define bad."

He looked at me, then nodded. "A lot of illegal things," he amended. "I've told a lot of lies, defrauded a lot of people out of money, cheated, stolen. Never killed anyone—"

I cleared my throat.

"Deliberately," he amended, "except in self-defence."

"That's a broad term," I said.

"No it's not. I got them before they got me."

"Yes, but—" I checked myself. "Sorry," I said. "We have a saying in our business, the customer is always right. Strictly speaking, preemptive defence is still defence. Of a sort. Besides, I don't make moral judgements."

He laughed. "Like hell you don't."

"No," I said. "I just execute them."

That sort of sobered him up a bit. "About the illegal stuff," he said. "I repented, years ago. And I haven't done anything like that since. I'm clean."

"You are indeed," I said. "You mended your ways and gave up illegal and antisocial activity, round about the time you made your big score and no longer needed the money. As far as we're concerned, you're fully redeemed and we have nothing against you."

He nodded. "Good," he said. "I'm glad about that."

He seemed sincere; which begged the question. So I asked it. "In which case," I said, "why exactly do you want to sell us your soul?"

He gave me a stern look; mind your own beeswax. "I just want to make sure," he said, "that as far as you're concerned, my soul's worth buying. You don't pay good money for something that's coming to you anyway."

"Indeed. And I'm here, ready and willing to do business. I trust that answers your query."

He nodded. "Just say it one more time, to humour me," he said.

"As far as we're concerned, you're the driven snow. All right?"

"Thank you." He paused; I think he was feeling tired. At his age, no surprise there. "The contract," he said.

"Ah yes." I took a gold tube from my sleeve and handed it to him. He hesitated before taking it, then pinched out the roll of parchment and spread it out. He used a flat glass lens to help him read; his own invention. Very clever. "You should go into business with that," I said.

He looked up. "What?"

"The reading lens. In a few centuries' time, everyone'll have one. You could make a fortune."

"I no longer need the money."

I shrugged. "Suit yourself. I was only trying to be helpful."

He clicked his tongue and went back to reading the contract. He moved his lips as he read, which surprised me.

Saloninus—well, you probably know this; after writing all those amazing books and inventing all that amazing stuff, he finally became rich as a result of discovering how to make synthetic blue paint. A great blessing to artists everywhere, and a dagger to the heart of the poor devils in Permia who used to make a precarious living mining lapis lazuli. It's a filthy job and the dust rots your lungs, but when the alternative is starvation, what can you do?

"This seems to be in order," he said. "Where do I sign?"

"Now just a moment," I said. "Are you sure you want to go through with this? It really does mean what it says. When you die—"

"I can read."

"Yes, but—" I hesitated. I have a duty to ensure that signatories understand the nature and meaning of their actions, and the inevitable consequences. I'm supposed to recommend that they take qualified independent advice first; but who could possibly be qualified to advise Saloninus?

Well. Me.

"If you sign this," I said, "you're going to go to hell. Which exists. And is not pleasant."

He looked at me. "I'd gathered that."

"Fine. So what on Earth do you think you're playing at? Why would you want to do such an incredibly stupid thing?"

He looked at me some more. Then he laughed.

~

He was such a funny little man. So conscientious.

I've had more than my share of bargaining with government. Most people will tell you it can't be done. Actually it can. True, they have absolute power; so what do they do? As often as not, they tie one hand behind their back. They strive to be fair, to be reasonable. I, of course, suffer from no such inhibitions.

"You say you've read my books," I said to him. "So, you tell me. Why would I want to do such an incredibly stupid thing?"

He went all thoughtful. "I suppose," he said, "that there's something you want which you sincerely believe is worth paying such a price for."

"Go on."

He looked so very uncomfortable. "You're seventy-seven years old," he said.

"Seventy-six."

"No, seventy-seven. I'm guessing you're conscious of the fact that you don't have all that much time left. I think that possibly you believe you're on to something—some fantastic new discovery, something like that—and only you would be able to make it, so it's no good leaving it to posterity to do the job, you've got to do it yourself. In desperation—"

"Excuse me."

"All right, not desperation. But resolved as you are to finish what you've started, you cast about for a way to gain yourself that extra time." He paused. "Am I close?"

I did my gesture of graceful acknowledgement. "In the blue."

"Two rings out."

"Close enough."

He steepled his fingers. It can be a dignified gesture betokening intelligence. I do it myself sometimes. It made him look like a clown. "Would you care to tell me what you're working on?"

I smiled at him. "No."

That displeased him. "I ask," he said, "not in any professional capacity but as your greatest fan."

"I don't want to spoil the surprise."

"Then in my professional capacity—"

I shook my head slightly. "I walk into your shop and ask to buy a twelve-inch double-edged knife. Do you ask me what I want it for?"

"Yes."

"No," I said. "You don't ask. You're selling, I'm buying. Or do you want to report back to your superiors and tell them you blew the deal?"

He gave me a funny little frown. "Why so secretive?"

"Why so inquisitive?"

"Uh-huh." Little shake of the head. "Bear in mind we know all about you, everything, every last indiscretion, every nasty little secret, everything you ever did when you were absolutely sure nobody was looking. And we aren't shocked. Nothing shocks us. We are incapable of disapproval. The only possible reason, therefore, for not telling us is that you're up to something."

I laughed in his face. "That's ridiculous."

"Is it?" he gave me a cool, level look. "You're a clever man, probably the cleverest who ever lived. And you're treacherous, and cunning, and entirely without scruple."

"I resent that. Bitterly."

"Oh come on. You proved there's no such thing as right and wrong."

"I have my own rules," I said. "I stick to them."

He breathed out slowly through his nose. A total sham, of course; he didn't breathe air. "I'm sorry," he said. "This has got to be the deal-breaker. Either you tell me what you have in mind, or I go to my superiors and tell them I can't trust you enough to contract with you."

(He'd never kept pigs, that's for sure. If he had, he'd have known how you get pigs into the cart, to take them to market. You can put a rope round their necks and pull till your arms get tired or you strangle the pig; they won't shift. They just keep backing away. They simply won't go in the direction you try and force them to go in. So the trick is, you try and drag them in the other direction, away from the cart. Next thing you know, they've backed away right up the ramp, and all you have to do is drop the tailgate.)

I held up my hands. "Really," I said, "there's no big secret. You were quite right. I wish to continue with my philosophical studies. I'm convinced I've found the key to a whole new way of understanding the universe, through scientific observation and mathematical representation. I believe the universe is a machine—a huge, complex machine, but no more than that. I believe that, given time, I can figure out how the machine works; not completely, of course, but to the extent where others will believe me and carry on the work. In doing so, I can free Mankind of the chains of superstition, cast down the false idols of Good and Evil, and allow the human race to grow uncramped, unfettered and undistorted by self-imposed restraints. If I can do this, my immortal soul is a small price to pay."

He squinted at me, as though I had the Invincible Sun standing directly behind me. "But you know that's garbage," he said.

"You said you liked my books."

"I do. I believe the stuff about conventional morality. I know it's true. I was on the team that set all that stuff up in the first place. But false superstitions and a completely mechanistic universe with no gods or devils—come on, look at me. I'm real. I exist. Therefore—"

I smiled at him. "I didn't say I believed it myself," I said.

I'd shocked him. You see? Not so unshockable after all.

"But that's beside the point," I went on. "The point is, given time and resources, I can prove my hypothesis, beyond all reasonable doubt." I paused. "Nobody else could, but I can. Because I'm Saloninus, the greatest ever. I can phrase arguments to make them unanswerable, I can bend the truth like hot steel until it's exactly the shape I want it to be. I can prove it so that future generations will believe it without question. They will follow my precepts and revere me, and my name will be on every man's lips and I shall live forever in their praises. The greatest philosopher, the wisest man who ever lived. Now, what more could an old, egotistical man want?"

His eyes were very wide. "That's insane."

"No, just extremely selfish."

"But millions of people will live by your teachings, die, and be damned to hell."

"Omelettes and eggs." I paused for effect. "And, from

your point of view, exceptionally good for business."

His lips moved noiselessly for a moment. Then he said, "I knew you were devious."

"And very, very selfish. And an artist, a creative. What could be better for an artist than to spin a fiction so convincing that it deceives the whole world?"

He shrank back a little. "You're up to something," he said.

"Yes. And I've just shared it with you. Now, do we have a deal?"

~

I wasn't always a philosopher.

I grew up on a farm, which is how come I know about pigs. My father was a big man who worried about everything. He worried about the sheep getting out, the bullocks poaching the ground in the top meadow, the rats spoiling the seed corn, the rain falling, the rain not falling, the wool price, and the looming threat of civil war. Worry leached every last grain of pleasure out of his life. The more he gained in his brief spells of prosperity, the more he worried about losing those gains. I never once knew him to enjoy a bright, clear spring morning or a sunset. He worried about me; as soon as it became apparent that I was smart, he worried about stifling my abilities and wasting my talents, so off I went, to school and then the Studium, and never came home again. He died while I was away, just before the war broke out and our farm was burned by General Aichmalote's retreating Sixth Army. None of the things he'd been afraid of came to pass in his lifetime, but all of them did shortly after his death. In a way, I think he missed out. If he'd lived another nine months, he'd have been proved right. As it was he died fretting his heart out that he'd frittered away his life in pointless anxiety.

My mother was a slender, elegant woman who'd worked in the leisure and entertainment industry. When I was a kid I could never figure out why the neighbours disapproved of her so much. After my father's death, she told me in a letter that he'd always been terrified she'd run off and leave him. He was wrong about that, she told me, left with a derelict farm, no livestock, and no money; I was never going anywhere, she wrote.

Many years later I settled my family's account with General Aichmalote; I forged evidence that led to him being executed for treason. He was guilty, as a matter of fact, but he'd covered his trail so well that there was no proof—boasted as much to me, thinking I was his friend and on his side—which gave me the idea in the first place. I'm an exceptionally good forger, though I say so myself. I take trouble with inks, paper, nib-shapes. (A hint for you: lawyers will sell you obsolete title deeds for a few coppers. Grind the writing off the parchment with brick dust, and you've got an irreproachably authentic vintage surface to write on. Nothing helps a lie succeed more than a generous helping of the truth.) I went to see the General in prison, the night before they cut his head off. He was utterly bewildered. "I know for damn sure I never wrote any of that stuff down," he said. "I know I'd never have been so stupid."

"You didn't," I said. "You have no reason to reproach yourself on that score." And then I told him what I'd done, and why. He took it badly; started howling vulgar abuse at me, whereupon I left in a huff. People can be so unreasonable.

I digress. My point is, I didn't inherit anything—nothing, not so much as a buckle. I'm a self-made, self-ruined man; my own achievement, my own fault. I didn't get my brains from my parents, and I most certainly didn't get any money. Query: if I'd had less brains and more money, would I have been happier? Answer: if a circle had four straight sides, wouldn't it be a square?

I'm my own property, to dispose of as I wish.

~

"Are you sure," he said, "you wouldn't rather have a lawyer read it through first?"

I was starting to feel tired. Old age; too much exertion, and I begin to fade. "Presumably," I said, "you're worried in case I try and get the agreement set aside on the grounds that I was rushed into it and didn't know what I was signing. Excuse me. You claim to have read my books. Whatever else I am, I'm not stupid, and I'm not senile, and I've read it and understood every word."

"And you're prepared to sign?"

"Yes."

He took the paper back from me. "Let me just have a quick look at that."

I grinned. Sensible; if there was a loophole I'd spotted, it'd be his fault. He read it carefully—I noticed he moved the tip of his forefinger along the lines—then stared at it for a while. "It's our standard form of contract," he said.

"Quite. Which has been used many times before, and on each occasion has proved lawyertight. Mind you, there's always a first time for everything."

Unkind of me to say that; he gave me a startled look, and read the whole thing over again. "In any case," I said, "I don't suppose you've got the authority to change anything without getting it cleared first."

"On the contrary, I have full—" He stopped, peered

at me as though I were a smeared window. "I just find it hard to accept," he said, "that someone I've admired and respected for so long would condemn himself to eternal damnation just so as to massage his own ego. It's such a stupid thing to do."

My turn to peer. But he looked genuinely concerned. "Honesty," I said.

"We're always honest. We always tell the truth."

I nodded. "If you can't trust the Father of Lies," I said. "Do you want me to sign the bloody thing, or not?"

⁓

"Of course I do," I said. "That's why I'm here."

He drummed his fingers on the desktop. "Fortunatus of Perimadeia," he said. "A man I've always looked up to. Caught one of your lot in a glass flask and heated him up over a hot flame until he turned into vapour. He wrote it up in his *Natural History.* Of course, the most fundamental thing about an experiment is that it's capable of producing the same result when repeated."

"Have you got a pen?" I asked. "If not—"

"Tisander of Scona, two centuries later," he went on, as if he hadn't heard me. "Tried to reproduce Fortunatus's results. The likeliest explanation is that he applied too much heat too quickly. They had to redraw several maps."

Tisander of Scona was new to me. Mind you, there are some things they don't want you to know about. "Sign the bottom of the page," I said, "and your initials at the foot of each paragraph."

He shrugged. "Will you be my principal liaison and point of contact? Paragraph three, section two."

"Yes."

"Splendid. I think we're going to get along famously."

~

Our standard form of contract—

Slightly amended to suit the specific requirements of the customer, but the core phraseology, the magic words that do the business, always stay the same—indefeasibly and absolutely devise and remit, in perpetuity, and so forth. In this case, we'd thrown in a guaranteed twenty years of healthy life, plus rejuvenation to age twenty-five. Apart from that, he was entitled to the usual package of benefits; access to limited specified supernatural powers through the agency of his designated case officer. That would be me.

"Not," he assured me, "that I'll be wanting any of the conjuring tricks. Cures for headaches and backaches, perhaps, and it would be nice to fly from library to library instead of having to walk or take the coach. But what I'm really after is something you couldn't possibly do for me. By definition."

Query: could there possibly be a mortal who's cleverer than Us? I filed the question with Department and got back the immediate reply *That remains to be seen.* Thank you so much.

"What you do with the benefits is entirely up to you," I said. "You can't make things worse for yourself by indulging your very basest desires, and you don't get credit for good works. In your shoes, I'd really let go, have as good a time as possible."

"I intend to." His eyes were cold and clear. "Do we need a witness?"

"That's me."

"Ah." I spread out the parchment, and in doing so knocked the cap of my inkwell off the desk onto the floor. "I wonder, could you possibly get that for me? I don't bend as easily as I used to."

By the time he'd straightened up I'd already signed. "There," I said. "All done."

He looked surprised, even shocked. "Splendid," he said.

∿

I took the parchment from him, rolled it up, and stuffed

it back in its tube. As easy as that.

"Right." He was smiling. "First the rejuvenation, and then do you think I could trouble you to show me all the kingdoms of the Earth?"

"No bother at all," I said, and rejuvenated him. His back straightened. His face sort of bubbled for a moment, as the surplus under his chin flowed upward to fill the sunken cheeks and the hollows under his eyes, stretching and smoothing the skin. Involuntarily he flexed his fingers as the arthritis and rheumatism dissipated; they lost that clawlike look, and the knuckles seemed to subside. His hair changed colour and sprouted back. He winced, as his missing teeth burst back up through their long-healed gums. "You might have warned me it'd hurt," he grumbled.

"So sorry," I said, and eased the pain away.

He was looking at his hands; first the backs, then the palms. "I never realised it had got so bad," he said.

"People don't. It's too gradual. And when a mortal looks in the glass, he never really sees what's there."

He acknowledged that with a slight tilt of the head. "The extraordinary thing," he said, "is how not-different it feels. More comfortable, but that's all. A bit like sleeping in your own bed again after a long time staying in inns." He looked at me. "You have done it properly, haven't you?"

I didn't bother to answer that. He stood up—lost his balance and wobbled for a moment, had to grab the edge of the desk—and peeled his clothes off. They were either too loose or too tight, depending on where they touched. "Good heavens," he said. "I haven't seen *that* in ages." He laughed. "Mind you, I've never let it rule my head. Still. I feel like turning somersaults."

"Be my guest."

He shook his head, grinning. "Out of practice," he said. "I might slip, land badly, and break my neck. Not that I need to worry about that anymore."

Yes, he'd read and understood the contract. Absolute immunity from any form of disease, injury, sudden death by homicide, accident, or misadventure. Paragraph 16 subclause (4) says that if he chooses to fight in battle I have to hold my invisible shield over him and protect him from the slightest scratch. If he cuts his own head off, I have to put it back on again. Every eventuality covered in absolutely unambiguous phrasing. Of course, we have all the best lawyers.

I conjured him raiment out of the air; he was entitled to one free outfit, like you get when you leave the army, or prison. I'd studied his tastes carefully, but there wasn't much of a common denominator. Most of his life he'd dressed in what he could afford, or steal, or had been given as a going-away present (see above), or had had bought for him by gullible patrons. I settled on a customary suit of solemn black, which favours most men of his (restored) age and build, particularly intellectuals, and is never out of style. He glanced down at the cuffs, then crossed his arms over his chest. "It fits," he said.

"Well, of course."

"I never had clothes that fitted when I was this age."

"Well, now you can afford the best. Anything else in the menswear line you have to pay for yourself, but I will of course issue you with infinite money on demand. I know," I added, as he raised an eyebrow. "That's bureaucracy for you. Never follow a straight line when a spiral will get you there eventually."

He cleared his throat and looked at me. Then he said, "All the kingdoms of the Earth, remember?"

"What? Oh, right, sorry. I was miles away."

~

In the absence of specific instructions from the customer I follow a standard itinerary; from the Republic to Scheria, Aelia, then Mezentia, the Mesoge, Perimadeia, follow the line of mountains to the Rhus, then due south to Blemya, quick tour of the Rosinholet and Cure Hardy khanates, up the River and back where we started from. It takes about four hours, unless the customer wants to stop and see anything in particular.

I was impressed by how well travelled he was. Every now and again he'd point down and say, "I was in prison there once" or "I slept rough in those woods for a fortnight." Over Scona he wanted to hover for a moment while he looked to see if the old *Grace & Endurance* was still there. It was. *Am I still barred from there?* he wondered. *Yes,* I told him, *you are.*

"You visit a lot of places when you're one jump ahead of the law," he told me. "Most of them don't hold particularly happy memories, I confess. Over there, look, that's where I got lynched by the investors in that fake silver mine thing. If the branch hadn't broken under my weight, I wouldn't be here now."

We were sailing high over the Dragon's Nest. I suggested lunch. He looked surprised. "Is it that time already?"

I pointed up at the noon sun. "I know a good place in Choris Anthropou," I said. "They do a passable spicy lamb with aromatic rice."

I don't eat, of course. I experience food, like I experience every other transitory thing, but I don't consume it and I can't taste it. The smell, however, creates tantalising shapes in my mind. It shouldn't do, but it does. Perhaps I've been down here too long.

"You're right," he said, stirring in a little plain yoghurt.

"It's really very good. We must come here again."

"Any time."

He frowned, a chunk of flatbread poised an inch from his mouth. "You're being really helpful," he said. "And considerate."

"Well, yes."

"You don't have to choose nice clothes for me and point out nice places to eat. It doesn't say you have to in the contract. It just says, you have to do what I tell you, within certain defined parameters."

I shrugged. "I try to make life pleasant for my customers," I said. "For the short period of time at their disposal."

"You don't have to."

"I like to."

He nodded. "There is no absolute right or wrong, good or evil, but there are good manners and common decency. Discuss."

"Have I got to?"

He waved his hand. "Figure of speech," he said with his mouth full. "Not a direct order. But I'd value your opinion, if you'd care to share it."

I thought for a moment. "There is no good or evil," I said. "There are only sides; the side you're on, and the other side." I paused. "You taught me that."

"So I did." He swallowed his chunk of bread. "I don't

think I ever believed that, but it was fun to argue and see if I could prove it. A lot of people think I did."

"Me included."

"Ah well."

"You're on one side," I said, "and I'm on another. At the moment, however, we aren't in conflict. Quite the reverse, we're in a contractual relationship, based on a mutual agreement, based on a shared wish to see a specific outcome. Therefore, at this stage, we're on the same side. Therefore, why shouldn't I be as helpful as I can?"

"You don't have to be."

I could see what he was getting at. "It's easier," I said. "It builds a smooth working relationship between us, making it easier for me to do my job."

"You don't have to be thoughtful. Or kind. You don't have to be good company."

I shrugged. "Most of my customers treat me with fear and loathing," I said. "I try and put them at their ease, but usually it's an uphill battle. You don't seem to be afraid of me or particularly disgusted by what I am. Why is that?"

"Don't change the subject," he said, "that's an order. You see, I don't think you understand the doctrine of sides one little bit. That, or you don't believe in it, but you're pretending you do, to flatter me."

I didn't say anything.

"The doctrine of sides," he went on, "states that there

is no right or wrong, only different perspectives. From where I stand, such and such a thing looks like a tree; from where you stand, it looks like a rock. For tree and rock, read sin and virtue."

"Yes, I got that part."

"Fine. But you're not judging me by the side I'm on. I'm the other side, but you're treating me like I were yours. The good man helps his friends and hurts his enemies. You aren't doing that. And the contract stuff is just sophistry. A contract's like that form of trial by combat in Scheria, where the two fighters are linked at the wrist with a chain. You should be trying to do me down."

"Why should I? Time will do it for me."

He was silent, and ate an olive. "You're making my allotted span as pleasant as possible so I won't notice how quickly it passes, thereby cheating me of time."

"If you care to look at it that way. If you'd prefer me to be aloof and nasty, I can do that for you."

He sighed, and threw his napkin on the table. "Take me to the Great Library of Mezentia," he said. "Philosophy section."

~

He was in there for about nine hours.

I offered to help him—fetch books, find places, look

things up—but he gave me a rather hostile look and said he could manage just fine, so I left him to it and tried to find something to amuse myself with.

In Mezentia, that's not so easy. Essentially it's a shoppers' town. If you want to buy things, there are no finer things to buy anywhere, often at sensible prices. The great streets—the Chandlery, Sheepfair, Tallowmarket, Stoneyards—are lined with establishments as well or better furnished and decorated than many a nobleman's house, in Aelia or the Republic. Insofar as there's beauty in useful, portable artefacts, Mezentia is the gallery of the world. Glassware, fabrics, metalwork useful and ornamental, porcelain, silverware—but their public art, although spectacular in scale, I find rather unsatisfactory. They're heavy on allegory, and the only patrons of the arts are the people who run the city, so you tend to get rather a lot of *Mezentia Wedded to the Sea* or *The Goddess Prosperity Embraces the Pewterers' Guild,* in marble, stuck up high so you have to crane your neck to see it. Since they're a proudly godless lot, the only religious art is strictly for export. They do excellent reproductions of all the great masterpieces; there are huge sheds down by the Wharf where hundreds of trained artisans crouch over benches, churning out the White Goddess of Beloisa all day every day. But it's art to buy and own, not to look at. You know what it looks like already.

You quickly become attuned to the customer. I felt him close his book and stand up, and sped back to the library steps, just as he was coming out. I smiled. "Useful session?"

"Very," he said. "Conjure me an army. I want to invade Mysia."

"I can do that for you," I said. "Out of interest, why?"

He didn't answer; that was me told. "To invade Mysia," I said, "the best starting point is the Butter Pass. Alternatively, you can follow the precedent of Calojan the Great and sail them up the Tonar on flat-bottomed barges. It takes longer, but you're more likely to get the element of surprise."

He scowled at me. "Let's do that, then."

~

Mysia is a dreary place, all forests and mud huts, though they do wonderful things with seafood. That's hardly a surprise, since the Tonar Delta has the finest oyster beds in the world, and the north coast is warmed by one of those big underwater currents. Mostly, though, people conquer Mysia because they're afraid someone else will conquer it first. Beating the Mysians isn't exactly difficult. The problem lies with recouping the cost of the invasion and occupation from an economy based on subsistence agriculture and nomadic livestock herding. Everybody who's anybody has invaded, stayed a year or so, and then gone resentfully home, wondering whose bright idea that was. It has more historic battlefield sites per square mile than anywhere else on Earth, apart from the Mesoge. The farmers plough up bones and sell them to the millers, for bonemeal; widely used in the metal-finishing industry.

We have our own armed forces, of course, but I assumed he wanted humans; so I enlisted the famous *condottier*, Alban of Bealfoir. I'd worked with him before; he's a good man.

"Of course I know Mysia," he said, over sea bass and sweet white wine in a palm-leaf-roofed teashop on the coast. "I led the annexation, four years ago. Two weeks' work, three in the rainy season. Have you got the money?"

Saloninus looked at me and I said, "Absolutely. My principals are footing all the bills."

Alban nodded. "That's all right, then," he said. "Your word's as good as cash in the bank." He turned back to Saloninus and said, "When would you like to start?"

"Immediately."

"That's not a problem." That's what I like about Alban, that can-do attitude. "I'll need seventy thousand nomismata up front, plus weekly instalments of forty thousand." He paused, then said, "Why?"

"Why what?"

"Why do you want to conquer Mysia?"

Saloninus sipped his wine, savouring the flowery aftertaste. "If you don't want the job, we can go elsewhere."

Alban held up both hands. "Sorry, sorry. Once we've taken the place, do you want to leave garrisons?"

Saloninus nodded. "I shall need a full army of occupation for at least forty years."

I frowned at that, but didn't say anything; not in front of the help. "I can arrange that," Alban said. "Obviously, you only need a fraction of the manpower for an occupation, unless you get an insurgency problem, which isn't likely here. That said—"

"They need to be paid, and the locals can't afford it," Saloninus interrupted. "Yes, I know that. We'll pay them, naturally."

"Say—" Alban took a moment for the dreams of avarice. "Thirty thousand nomismata a year?"

Well, it's not my money, so I kept quiet. "Fine," Saloninus said indifferently. "I'll put a lump sum in escrow with the Knights, as a token of good faith; draw on it as you need it."

I think the poor man was seriously shaken. He's straightforward enough for a man in his line of work, but I'm guessing that *draw on it as you need it* undermined the very core of his understanding of the world. All those years killing people and beating them up in order to get money, and instead, there are people out there who'll just give it to you. "Suits me," he said, in a quiet voice. "Right. First thing in the morning." He paused. I surreptitiously conjured a small steel-reinforced chest under my right foot. "Here," I said, and pushed it toward him under the table.

He wouldn't need to count it. He knew that. He rested his foot delicately on it, as if on a rose.

~

Same old same old for the villagers and nomads of Mysia. Out of the early morning mists emerged a column of armoured men, their footsteps barely audible on the thick leaf mould. King Carduan IV wasn't at home when we called; he never is when people invade his kingdom. He has barges moored ready all the time, with the royal treasury stowed aboard. He's not bothered about anybody stealing it. After so many wars and occupations, there's not enough there to make it worth the effort. The royal guard stayed home, their wives busily weaving baskets to sell to the foreigners.

Our forces occupied the Citadel. It's an amazing thing, if you like military architecture (I must confess I do, though purely on an aesthetic level). It was built by the Eastern Empire, back when they were the invaders du jour. They chose a flat-topped mountain, actually a dormant volcano; there's a rainwater lake up there on top, natural hot water. The defensive walls are built out of huge rectangular blocks of black lava; fifteen feet thick at the base. There's a curtain wall, a boiling—seriously—moat, an outer wall, and an inner keep. There's fifteen acres of storage sheds for food and equipment. The circumference of the curtain wall is three miles, but four hundred men could hold it indefinitely against the world, assuming they've laid in adequate supplies. It won't come as a surprise to learn that the Citadel has never been taken, by storm, siege, or treachery. Come to that, it's never been attacked. It's been voluntarily evacuated and abandoned nine times, but that's different.

He got me to fill the barns with sacks of flour and barrels of salted bacon, while Alban's sappers made a few minor repairs to the drawbridge. The Mysians don't come near the place ever, except to loot the food stores when an invader leaves. They know it's nothing to do with them. Also, I think they know it's a volcano, a fact which appears nowhere in the military libraries of the surrounding nations.

Alban kept trying to report to me for orders, even though he knew perfectly well who was in charge. He was trying to make himself believe this was a normal, businesslike military operation, and that he wasn't working for a lunatic. "Do you anticipate any hostile activity from the King?" he asked me.

I shook my head. "Usually when there's an invasion he goes and stays with his cousin the seed-merchant, just across the border," I said. "I gather he prefers it there to here. The Mysians won't bother you at all. Particularly if you buy their baskets."

He nodded. "What are we doing here?"

"Don't ask me."

The customer is always right; if we had a physical headquarters, that would be written up on the wall in golden letters. But you can't help speculating. Why would a man want to invade a country? The primeval will to power, maybe, or perhaps he likes watching the way blood changes colour when it soaks away into the dust. A philosopher? He might want to observe the changes that absolute power made to his personality—does it corrupt absolutely, or can the philosopher-king control it and bend it to his will? An opportunity to create the perfect society; I considered and rejected that, because if that was what you had in mind, you wouldn't try and do it in Mysia. Or perhaps he'd played with toy soldiers as a boy, or years ago a Mysian kicked sand in his face on a beach somewhere. You just don't know, with humans. There is no wrong or right, except for the eternal, unchangeable rightness of the customer.

Mine not to reason why. Not my place.

"You've got to tell me," I said to him. "It's driving me crazy. What are we doing here?"

He looked up from a huge scale plan of the Citadel. He'd been going over it for hours, making tiny notes in red and green ink; improvements in the defences. I'd peeked over his shoulder a few times. They were brilliant. He should've been a military engineer. Belay that; Mankind, thank your lucky stars he was never a military engineer.

"Excuse me?"

"You know exactly what I mean. Why did we invade this country? Why are we here?"

"Oh, that." He carefully dried the nib of his pen on a scrap of cotton waste before laying it down, so it wouldn't splodge the plans. "I'd have thought you'd have figured that out for yourself by now."

He had the only chair. I sighed and sat down on the floor. "I've tried, believe me. But I can't."

"Keep trying," he said. "It's dogged as does it."

I'm ashamed to say I jumped up and banged the desk with my fist. He gave me a pained look. "You want me to tell you?"

"Yes."

"Ah well." He leaned back in his chair. It had been

the seat of twelve consecutive garrison commanders, and the arms were scarred by fingernails picking at the carved edges. "It's a bit of a sideshow, really."

"Is it?"

"Oh yes. It's just that I want Mankind to be in a suitably receptive frame of mind, for when my great hypothesis is published. You may disagree, but my personal experience is that when you're trying to concentrate on the higher metaphysical and ethical issues, things like hunger, poverty, and the constant threat of violent disruption really don't help at all. Get rid of them, therefore, and they'll be that much more willing to listen and easier to persuade."

I looked at him. "Get rid of them," I repeated.

"Yes, why not? And that's what we're doing here." He winked at me. "That's a hint," he said. "A great big one. Now, if you don't mind, I'm trying to get some work done."

Disturbing the customer's concentration when he's engaged in his chosen task is explicitly forbidden in the contract; so I didn't talk to him again until he'd finished for the day, rolled up his plans, closed his books, and put his feet up on the desk. Only then did I take him in a light supper and a glass of white wine.

"Here's what I think," I said. "Mysia is bordered by three powerful, militaristic nations. For centuries, all three have lived in terror of one of the others seizing Mysia and using it as a springboard for invasion. In consequence, they've spent a grossly large proportion of their national wealth on defence, anticipating what they see as the inevitable aggression; their kings have taxed their feudal barons to the point where all three countries are on the edge of economic collapse and revolution and civil war are a distinct possibility, but the foreign threat refuses to go away so long as Mysia remains independent and weak."

He gave me a faint smile, which I found patronising.

"Your idea," I went on, "is a Mysia that's independent and *strong*. Once the three great nations come to understand that Mysia can no longer be conquered, they'll realise that war isn't inevitable. In fact, since any enemy would have to pass through Mysia to get to them, and Mysia is strong and independent, war is actually impossible. So, with a vast sigh of relief, they stop bleeding themselves dry with defence spending; the people prosper, prosperity brings content, there's no more talk of revolution, and everybody is happy and peaceful. Since the three nations dominate the civilised world, happiness and peace become general throughout Mankind." I paused for breath. "You think you're so clever."

"I am so clever."

"Yes." I hesitated. Not my place. The customer, and so

on. Even so. "It's not going to work, you know."

"Isn't it?"

"Of course not. We've got a thousand years of case law on our side. If you sell us your soul in return for a chance to do good, it makes absolutely no difference whatsoever. A contract is a contract. The higher courts will not intervene."

He laughed. "I know *that*," he said. "I'm not stupid."

I looked at him. Usually I'm so good at reading faces. "You're up to something."

He lifted the lid off the plate I'd brought him; pan-fried liver in a cream and white wine sauce. "Whatever gives you that idea?" he said.

～

Bless his suspicious little heart.

Consider mortality. Man that is born of woman hath but a short time to live, and awareness of this crucial brevity tends to concentrate his mind. Immortals are under no such constraint. True, they have so much longer in which to acquire and assimilate data, but far less incentive to get on with the job of processing it, assessing and analysing, forming hypotheses, and reaching conclusions. They have infinite time in which to stop and smell the flowers; furthermore, for them there is nothing to gain and nothing to lose. Change and decay, however, is in all around we see, and this prompts us to think harder, faster, and more clearly. That's my take on it, anyway. Maybe they're just not as smart as we are.

I first became interested in Mysia when I read the bit about the ants in Peregrinus's *Geography*—you know, about how the Mysians train ants to dig for gold; the ants burrow into the earth and come back up with specks of gold dust clinging to their legs, which the Mysians carefully brush off with the pin-feather of a woodcock. It reminded me of something else I'd read, about a gold mine in Blemya where the dust was so close to the surface that the grass grew up through it and forced it to the surface; and that mine was well documented and real.

I couldn't do anything about it at the time, as I was on the run in Antecyra, sleeping rough in a derelict dovecote and stealing pigswill to eat. But as soon as I was back in a place with libraries, I started to read everything I could lay my hands on about Mysia, and gradually it all started to come together. Rusty brown and greenish yellow rocks, beds of porphyry, bits of stone brought back by travellers with a distinctive honeycomb look about them, accounts of dried-up riverbeds and lava fields; all of them connected to one particular place, the mountain range in the middle of which the Empire had built the Citadel.

I searched the Imperial archives at Rosh Roussel. The military surveyors had chosen the site on purely strategic grounds, but that might just mean they were unobservant, or ignorant. Buried in the survey notes I found references to gold nuggets found in dried-up watercourses, together with strict instructions from the commander-in-chief to hush up such finds and discourage off-duty prospecting; the last thing they wanted was the garrison deserting en masse to go gold prospecting.

What with one thing and another, I never had time or liberty to go to Mysia; not until I made my big score in the paint trade, at which point I lost interest in get-rich-quick projects, settled down, and got disgracefully old. But I never stopped being interested. If only I were fifty years younger, I kept telling myself. And then, quite suddenly, I was.

No problem finding excuses to go strolling in the hills around the Citadel, unobserved by my servant/keeper. I couldn't very well take a pick and shovel with me; luckily, I didn't need them. Peregrinus was right after all; there was gold dust to be found in the anthills, kick them over with your toe and there it was, glittering in the sun.

Query: why had nobody else found it? Quite simple, really. The Mysians aren't interested in gold, never have been. Their currency and medium of exchange is fine woollen cloth. As for invading soldiers, they were under orders not to stray too far from the Citadel, lest they be caught and eaten by the savages.

A few cursory inspections led me to what I'd known all along I'd eventually find. At first I couldn't believe it, so I smuggled out a few tools. I didn't have to dig very far.

The two low, plump, free-standing hills half a mile from the Citadel, the ones the Imperial surveyors nick-named the Cow and Calf, are solid gold. Two enormous nuggets, with a bit of peat and cooch-grass on top.

And, best thing of all, *he* didn't know about them. No-body did; except me.

~

He was up to something, and I had no idea what it was.

It did occur to me that maybe he was after the vast gold deposits buried under the mountains nearby; but no, it couldn't be that. If he'd wanted unlimited gold, all he'd have had to do was ask me; no need for soldiers and invasions. Besides, what good would gold be to him, in his situation? One truth abides, and overshadows all the rest—you can't take it with you. And it's not like gold's any good for anything except as a source and reposi-tory of wealth. You'd have to be desperately, profoundly stupid to trade your immortal soul for mere purchasing power. So, clearly, it wasn't that.

I can't pretend I was enjoying Mysia. "Cultural desert" doesn't begin to do it justice. Generally speaking, whenever a certain number of humans congregate in one place, they tend to generate art in some form or another, even if it's just whittled bones and splodges of ochre on the cave wall. And all human art (tautology; all art is human; it's the only thing we omnipotents can't do) has merit, if you look at it long enough and closely enough. Except in Mysia. The Mysians don't sculpt or paint, they don't scratch incuse decorations on the handles of their axes, they don't even tattoo their bodies or weave fish bones into their hair. Having no gods, they carve no idols. There is no word for artist in the Mysian language; instead there's a long-winded periphrasis that translates as man-who-deceives-others-into-giving-food-by-spoiling-bits-of-wood.

Well; I've been in deserts before, sand deserts and ice deserts, landscapes of volcanic rock, bleak plateaux blasted clean of life by war and weapons you couldn't begin to imagine. On such occasions, I seek solace in a good book. But that was one thing I simply couldn't do in Mysia. It came as something as a shock to me when I realised it. All my favourite books were either written by Saloninus, or commentaries on, rejections of, or defences of his works and theories. And here I was, shackled by chains of contract to the man himself. I remember opening my battered old copy of *Human, All Too Human* and glancing down at the so-familiar text, and thinking, I can't accept any of this anymore. I felt utterly betrayed, bereft, and destitute.

I know, you shouldn't allow what you know of the artist as a man to influence your view of his work. Take music. Jotapian was a horrible person, a drunkard who beat his wife and scarred his children for life with his atrocious behaviour. Mavortis's views on women and people with dark skin were simply loathsome. And the greatest of them all, Procopius—it takes quite a bit to shock me, as you can imagine, but he does, to the core. So; the knowledge that Saloninus was treacherous, insincere, devious, mercenary—I knew all that, and it had never fazed me before. But actually meeting him, spending every waking moment with him, was different. I have to say, the sense of loss was overwhelming. No, I didn't enjoy Mysia. Not one bit.

～

"Guess what," he said to me. "There's gold in them thar hills."

He'd come back from one of his early morning tramps. I should've accompanied him, but he didn't ask me to and I'm not at my best in the mornings. "Is that right?" I said.

He nodded happily. "This is the most amazing stroke of luck," he said. Then he paused. "I'm assuming it's luck," he added. "Or have you been helping and neglected to tell me?"

I assured him I had nothing to do with it. He shrugged. "Makes no mind," he said. "You do realise, this makes everything so much easier. It solves the one problem I hadn't got around to dealing with."

He sat down on a folding stool on the verandah of the lookout post he'd taken to using as an office. It had a splendid view of the mountains. I brought him a cup of jasmine tea and a plate of honeycakes; his favourite. "What problem?" I asked.

"You know perfectly well," he said. "In twenty years' time I won't be here and you'll stop funding the garrison. At that point, the soldiers will go away and there'll be the most almighty war, as the three nations scramble to grab Mysia. The whole scheme will founder and everything will go wrong. You foresaw that, naturally."

"Well, yes."

He laughed, and slapped me rather hard on the back. "Well," he said, "now that won't happen. There's enough gold in the hills here to hire every mercenary soldier in the world. Which," he added cheerfully, "is what we're going to do."

I felt as though I'd just walked into an invisible wall. "Are we? Why?"

"What we're going to do," he went on, "is turn Mysia into a genuine, functional pirate kingdom. We'll send out the word to all the nations of the Earth. Give us your vermin, your scum, your huddled masses yearning to breathe free, the wretched refuse of your teeming shores. The mountains are made of pure gold; all you have to do is hack it out, smelt it down, and spend it." He grinned so wide I thought his face would split. "What's even better than an independent, strong Mysia? An independent, strong, *malignant* Mysia, the sump and abscess of the known world, something the civilised nations can unite against but never actually defeat. They'll mount crusades against it, they'll blockade it, lay it under permanent siege; every nation will send its best fighting men to join the glorious cause. But it won't do a bit of good, because of the impregnable castle and the gold. It's a basic tenet of military science. No stronghold can be taken if a mule laden with gold bars can leave it unobserved. Did I mention these hills are honeycombed with caves and tunnels?"

"No. Besides, they aren't."

He looked at me. "They will be," he said, "in the next five minutes. That's an order."

I sighed. His wish, my command. Actually, it was a

tricky one; how to riddle a mountain with wormholes without the whole lot collapsing, and in such a way that the besieged can get out but the besiegers can't use the tunnels to get in. It took me forty-five seconds to figure out how it could be done. Practically an eternity.

"Well?"

"All done," I told him. "Do you want detailed schematics?"

"Yes."

"On your desk," I said. "In sealed brass tubes."

He smiled. "Thank you," he said. "Well, I call that a good morning's work. Of course," he went on, "if there hadn't been gold there already, I'd have had to make you put it there, so it's all as broad as it's long, strictly speaking. But this way, I've saved you a job."

"Thank you so much," I said.

I left him to his tea and cakes and slouched back to the Citadel, to oversee the installation of the five giant trebuchets he'd ordered. I was deeply troubled. Not in itself unusual; but I had a distinct feeling that I'd missed something. That's not a normal or comfortable feeling for me. I don't miss things. Like I said, I live and have my being in the detail. Also, if I had that feeling, it was because I was meant to. It was as though he'd put up a big painted sign saying UP TO SOMETHING and was sitting directly beneath it.

I dug out my copy of the contract and read it over, for the umpteenth time. The words hadn't changed since I last looked at them. There they still were, as airtight and lawyerproof as they'd always been. When he died, he'd be ours. Until then, he could have anything he wanted. A wonderfully straightforward document, its phrasing a miracle of functional elegance, as close to a work of art as we're capable of getting.

So, then, the big unanswered question: why bother to dig gold out of the ground when he could have all the gold he wanted for the asking?

~

The bad guys started to arrive.

It sounds ridiculous coming from me, but the sight of evil en masse is one I find disturbing. They came by the shipload and the cartload; mostly men, of course; mostly from cities. Some came in groups, heavily armed and ferociously suspicious. Some drifted in singly—desperate rather than actively wicked, most of the singletons were. I think the majority of them were more concerned with a few free meals than the prospect of unlimited wealth. Because the Citadel is so vast, we had plenty of accommodation, and my organisation provided the food and the beer. There were any number of loud, angry meetings in the Great Hall, with passionate, violent men demanding to know what the catch was, and Saloninus repeating, over and over again, there isn't one. The more he asserted it, the less they believed him, which is human nature for you. Within days of the establishment of the Commune, as we decided to call it for want of a better name, I was aware of half a dozen conspiracies to overthrow the government by force and take control; they all foundered, of course, as soon as they faced the fact that there was no government to overthrow and no control to take. All they could've done to assert their personalities would have been to slaughter the cooks—who, being undead, wouldn't have minded in the least—but it never happened because nobody could be bothered.

The first thing they all wanted to know, of course, was *Where's the gold?* And I would point to the hillside, and tell them where they could be issued with picks, shovels, buckets, all free of charge. There was a lot of grumbling about backbreaking hard labour, my mother didn't raise me to be no miner, and so forth. But hardly any of them left on that score. The work was too easy. It literally was a case of scuff off a few inches of turf and help yourself. I'd expected that a minority would gang up to rob the diggers, but it didn't happen; more trouble and effort than it was worth. As a community, apart from a few drunken stabbings, we had something approaching a zero crime rate. I found that seriously disturbing, as you can imagine.

"What *are* you up to?" I asked him, one night after dinner. "Go on, you can tell me."

He smiled and patted me on the arm. "Bear up," he said. "Only nineteen years and nine more months to go." He poured himself a glass of wine; instinctively started to offer me one, realised. "When it's all over and I've gone where I'm going," he said, "will you come and visit me?"

I looked at him. I felt embarrassed. "If you like," I said.

"I'd really appreciate that," he said. "It'd be rather less daunting if I knew there'd be a friendly face."

What could I possibly say?

~

I guess the other thing that was getting me down was not having very much to do. Usually when I'm on an assignment I hardly have time to breathe; bring me gold, bring me rubies, bring me the severed heads of my enemies, bring me the most beautiful woman in the world. Nothing but rush and scurry, and when you're run off your feet, you don't have time to brood. But once the bad guys were all nicely settled in, I wasn't really needed for anything. Saloninus more or less boarded himself up in that shed he'd taken such a liking to, with piles of books and papers and mathematical instruments and alembics and astrolabes and retorts and flasks and who knows or cares what; when I asked if there was anything I could do to help, he scowled at me and yelled, yes, piss off and let me concentrate. Which left me at a loose end, somewhere I'm not comfortable being.

If only certain proverbs were true. I had idle hands, but nobody found work for them to do. I couldn't catch up on my paperwork, because I'm always punctilious about writing up my logs and filing my reports as I go along. Mysia being Mysia, and reading being out of the question, all I could occupy myself with was long walks in the hills (I hate walking in the country, particularly up-hill) and tearing myself apart trying to figure out what he was up to. Not a happy time for me, I have to say.

Then one day—I guess it was about a year after we arrived in Mysia—he called me in to his shack. You can tell how demoralised I'd become; I didn't even remember to provide jasmine tea and honeycakes. I sat down on an upturned crate and looked at him mournfully. "What can I do for you?"

He smiled. "You're bored, aren't you?"

"Is it that obvious?" I sighed. "I'm sorry. I won't let it show in future."

He waved the apology away. "I'm the one who should be sorry," he said. "I'm being inconsiderate. Major fault of mine, so people tell me, I just don't think about others, only myself."

"That's all right," I said warily.

"Anyway." He clapped his hands together. "I've got a job for you."

I was ashamed of how pathetically grateful I was to hear him say that. "Your wish is my command, master. What can I do for you?"

He handed me a sheet of paper. "I want you to get these people and bring them here. Offer them so much money they won't be able to refuse. Then find somewhere comfortable for them to work."

On the paper were the names of all the greatest living painters, sculptors, and architects in the world. My heroes, every one of them. "These people," I stammered. "What are you going to do with them?"

"I fancy being a patron of the arts," he said with a chuckle. "So give them anything they want, whatever it takes to help them produce their finest work. All right?"

Stunned doesn't begin to cover it. "Of course," I said. "My wish—I mean, your wish—"

"You already said that. Get on with it."

A significant slip of the tongue. My wish; my greatest, most fervent wish—to see art again, beautiful and wonderful works of art, the one thing I and my kind can't do, but humans can. As soon as the angel choirs stopped singing inside my head, I asked him. "Why?"

"Get on with it," he repeated. "And go away. I'm working."

~

I had no trouble at all persuading them to come. They fell, as all artists and creative people do, into two well-defined categories: those who desperately needed money, and those who were desperately afraid they'd be needing money very soon, even though they were temporarily solvent. I suspect I could've got them for far less than I actually paid, but I didn't want to. Not my money, after all, and there's something rather special about seeing pathetic gratitude in the eyes of men you admire.

I had studios built for them in the high turrets of the Citadel, so they could revel in the light. Special cranes to lift colossal blocks of marble. The richest, rarest pigments—none of Saloninus's synthetic blue for my boys, nothing but the purest lapis lazuli and carnelian, flown direct from the mountains and arid deserts of Permia by overworked demons. I even—not without some misgivings, since I was a respectable majordomo, not a pimp—arranged for a supply of inspiration; the painters, after all, had to paint something, and when I told them to use their imaginations, they just looked at me. So Inspiration arrived in a long train of covered coaches, which meant yet more work for me—changes to the plumbing, that sort of thing. And, since the last thing I wanted was the artists getting into fights with the cutthroats and murderers, there had to be plenty of inspiration to go round.

"In fact," someone said to me, as we stood watching the roof being put on yet another magnificent new extension to the Palace of Beauty, "what you're building here is the ideal republic."

I looked at him. He was quite possibly the finest icon-painter of his generation, a small, bald man with a limp. "What?" I said.

"You've got everything," he said. "Unlimited wealth means infinite leisure, a prerequisite for contemplation of the truly worthwhile. Your strong and well-respected warrior caste ensure total security. A happy and contented underclass grow all the food, which they sell for inflated prices to the better sort. As for them, you couldn't ask for a more suitable set of founding fathers for a great nation; fearless warriors, artistic geniuses, and women specially selected for their beauty, charm, and ability to get on with all different sorts of people. All under the benign, feather-light governance of a genuine philosopher-king. Come back in a hundred and twenty years, this country will be populated by a race of supermen."

Now that rang a bell: *I give you the superman; man is something to be overcome.* Saloninus in his rare poetic vein. "You think so?"

He laughed. "Look at Aelia," he said. "Founded by convicts transported for nameless crimes from their native land. Or take the old Empire. That all started with a band of outlaws and bandits who stole a load of women from a nearby city. Their offspring went on to conquer the world. Of course, you've got a much better situation here, seeing as how you're strategically poised to dominate the three great nation-states of the civilised world. I don't much like the term 'manifest destiny,' but it's hard to think of another way of putting it."

Up to something, I said to myself under my breath, and went to see Saloninus.

"But my dear fellow," he said, "you've got it completely wrong. I did it for you."

That walking-into-an-invisible-wall feeling again. "You what?"

"For you," he repeated. "I could see how bored you were, and I know how much you like art. So I sent you out for some artists." He smiled. "And it worked. You've been so much happier these last few months."

That I couldn't deny. "For me?" I repeated idiotically.

"Why not? It didn't cost me anything and it's given you pleasure."

"Yes, but—" My mouth sort of seized up. You can't work closely with a man for nearly two years and not learn something about him. I was as sure as anyone ever can be; he was telling the truth. "Why?"

"Excuse me. I don't understand."

"Why would you do something just for me?"

He sighed. "Oh dear," he said. "I thought we'd got past all that. Sit down, put your feet up for a moment. Go on, that's an order."

I have to obey orders. I sat down, and put my feet up. "The fact is," he said, "you're not a bad person. You work for Evil, but as a—well, I can't say *as a human being;* as an entity, you're a normal, decent individual with a basically kind heart and an appreciation of the finer things. You can't deny that, it's true."

I frowned. "We're on different sides."

"No, we're not. For the next seventeen years and ten months we're on my side. After that—" He shrugged. "What am I supposed to do, be nasty to you all the time? I haven't got the energy. You know what they say, it takes seventeen muscles to smile and forty-three to frown. I only have a limited time at my disposal, I've got work to do. I can't waste time and effort on counterproductive friction and hostility."

I felt like I was being overwhelmed by a great wave. "But the outcome," I said. "The ideal society."

He shook his head. "I told you to hire some artists," he said. "You were the one who built all the palaces and studios for them. Also, you were the one who shipped in all the whores. Splendid idea, by the way, I'm not criticising. Nevertheless, the fact remains: if the result of all this is a race of superior human beings, if it's anyone's doing it'll be yours, not mine."

⌒

My blood can't run cold because I have no blood. Just as well.

I'm permitted to do small, unobtrusive acts of goodness. Well, strictly speaking I'm not, but a blind eye is generally turned when I give small sums of money to struggling artists and street musicians, when I'm off duty, because such acts of kindness are trivial and without lasting consequences. It's one of the small perks I get for having to spend my life in the field, among humans. But there's a world of difference between that and taking a decision that could—who am I trying to kid; that will inevitably lead to the ideal society, the race of superior human beings. He was quite right, of course. He hadn't said anything about female companionship, for the artists or the cutthroats. That had been my idea.

He doesn't like people talking about it, but Saloninus

once wrote an opera. He needed the money, is his excuse. I have no reason to disbelieve and not forgive.

In the culminating scene (it's actually quite good, for opera) the intellectual sort-of-chorus character who's been watching the drama unfold congratulates the protagonist; how wonderful, he says, your luck's turned out to be. Look, there are your enemies, slaughtering each other for something you already discarded.

Just thought I'd mention that, as an insight into the way his mind worked.

I had two options. I could report what I'd done to my superiors and throw myself on their mercy.

Exactly. So I did the other thing. I kept quiet about it, did nothing, stood idly by and allowed the disaster to unfold. There was, after all, the very real chance that nobody would ever figure out that it had been my fault. Great nations and ideal societies do emerge from time to time, after all; by accident, by chance, through the agency of natural evolution. The examples my artist friend had mentioned, for instance; Aelia was nobody's *fault,* and neither was the old Empire—and besides, once they'd passed their zenith and fallen into decadence and decay they were no problem to anyone—very good for business, in fact, from our perspective. And our lot may be all-seeing and all-knowing, but that's a long way removed from all-understanding. There was even the remote possibility that the founding of the New Mysia wasn't my fault or an accident but in fact part of some grand overarching plan by our opposite numbers in the organisation, which I simply didn't know about—and that's what you get for being out of the office most of the time and never reading the memos.

But I couldn't help wondering. Was that what he'd been up to, or was it something else? Could he have foreseen that I'd have exceeded my discretion to that small, disastrous extent? Am I that predictable? Was he that devious?

~

"I've been thinking," I said. "Maybe we should send the women away. After all, this is supposed to be a mining colony, not a cathouse."

He shook his head. "It was supposed to be a garrison," he pointed out. "The miners and the artists more or less just happened. And you can't send the girls home now, there'd be riots. And besides, they're happy here, they've got a much better life than they ever had back in the cities. No, they can stay." My face must've betrayed me, because he frowned. "My mind's made up," he said. "Sorry if it offends your puritan sensibilities."

"But the unforeseen consequences—"

"What consequences?"

"I don't know, I can't foresee them."

He sighed and patted me on the shoulder. "Don't worry about it," he said. "That's your problem, you're always worrying. You can't enjoy life if you're a worrier. I know you're concerned about this ideal society thing, but who knows, it may never happen. Nothing's set in stone, you know. Now push off and admire some paintings, while I get on with some work."

~

I felt sorry for him, but what can you do?

Besides, I had other things on my mind. The passage of time, for one thing. My simple ruse for getting him out from under my feet had succeeded beyond my wildest dreams—it had never occurred to me that it would be so easy—but I still had the work itself to do, and it wasn't going as well as I'd hoped.

You probably don't know about my brief, inglorious career in alchemy. It's a segment of my life I've tried to underplay, because nobody likes to admit failure. At one stage I felt I might possibly be on to something, but stuff kept getting in the way—I had endless trouble with patrons, and then I sort of murdered my wife, and I blew up my laboratory, and then I had to leave town in a hurry. So

I never found out if the last experiment I'd set up actually came out right in the end. For reasons I won't bore you with, I had to get out while it was still in progress, leaving the big question unanswered: had I succeeded in turning base metal into gold, or hadn't I?

(Actually, it wasn't murder, though it felt like it. I warned her not to drink the stuff, but she drank it anyway. I still feel guilty about that, even though it's one of the very few bad things that have happened in my lifetime that wasn't really my fault.)

Since all my notes had gone up in flames, along with my workshop and the royal palace, I had to go back to first principles and start again. I had assumed that wouldn't be a problem; I was clever then, I still was clever, piece of cake. But I'd discounted the crucial element of luck, serendipity, call it what you will. Back then, I'd stumbled across vital conclusions or reached them through flashes of intuition. That didn't seem to be happening this time around. I wondered what was different. The conclusion I came to was that my circumstances were too easy. Admittedly I had damnation waiting for me seventeen years down the line, but I couldn't make myself panic about something so relatively distant. The first time, I'd either been desperately short of money or running late on a king's deadline, with the noose or the block just a day or so away. I'm guessing my brain needs the special extra stimulus of rank terror to kick it into a higher gear. And that, of course, was missing.

Alchemy is simple stuff, really. The world we know is made up of components, very small ones. The smaller you go, the more interchangeable these components are. If you go right down, really, really small, it's theoretically possible to exchange one lot of components for another. And that's alchemy.

Of course I'm exaggerating, simplifying and bending the truth. If it were as easy as that, anyone could do it. There's also the not-so-trivial matter of the world we don't know; the things we don't know are there, the consequences we can't foresee. The harder I worked, the more of that sort of thing I seemed to come up against. I didn't like that. I'm used to everything coming easily. Usually, I just sit down and concentrate and it all comes gushing out; I scrape away a bit of turf, and there's the gold, a few inches under the surface. Rolling up my sleeves and digging isn't what I'm used to, and I sort of resent having to do it. Silly of me, but that's my nature.

Keeping secrets from the All-Seeing isn't as hard as it sounds. The key is making sure they don't correctly interpret what they see. Simple misdirection; the street corner conjurer's stock-in-trade. I don't care how mighty or sublime they are, if they've got a personality, they can be understood; if they can be understood, they can be deceived. If they can be deceived, I can deceive them. What can I say? It's a gift. I was born with it. God-given, you might call it.

But nothing lasts forever, not even the spell I weave. Sooner or later, he was bound to find out what I was up to in my damp, cold little shack. I'm guessing it was the thin plume of smoke; even the finest charcoal isn't entirely smokeless. I'd been planning to pretend it was just the stove, but since it was freezing cold in there (had to be, for sound alchemical reasons), that wasn't likely to fool him for long.

I remember the scene as though it were yesterday. He stood in the doorway of the shack, staring at my modest array of alchemical equipment, his face grey as slate. "May I ask," he said in a thin, strained voice, "what you're doing?"

"Certainly you may. I'm just trying to reproduce an experiment. As you know, the essential quality of a successful experiment is that it should be capable of being—"

"Fortunatus of Perimadeia."

I looked away. "No," I said.

"Don't lie to me," he screamed; I confess, I was shocked. "Don't you ever dare lie to me."

"I'm not lying," I said calmly. "This experiment was designed by Fortunatus's teacher and mentor, Sedulius of

Ligois. True, Fortunatus later elaborated on it, but—"

"I'm not going in that thing. You can't make me."

I turned and faced him. "Actually, I can," I said gravely. "I can order you to get inside my alembic, and you'd have no choice but to do as you're told. But since I have no intention of doing any such thing, I really don't see what all the fuss is about."

He backed away until he was on the other side of the doorframe. "Alchemy is forbidden," he said. "It's a black art."

"Oh come on," I said gently.

"It is. It's unnatural. It's attempting to transform that which has been created into something else. It's the worst possible sin. I'm going to have to report this."

Who to, I didn't ask. "This isn't that kind of experiment," I told him. "This is just an improved method of extracting nitre from everyday organic materials. If it works, it means vastly improved crop yields in areas of marginal agricultural value."

"What?" He stared at me. "Why? Whatever for?"

I sighed. "Look behind you," I said. "Mountains. Scrub. If this miserable country's going to be self-sufficient in food, we need to do something about it." Then I frowned. "What did you think I was doing?"

He came a step or two back into the shack and sniffed; his long, delicate nose detecting and analysing the contents of the alembic. "Chicken manure."

"A rich natural source of nitre."

"You're boiling up chickenshit."

"Yes. But a hundred and sixty per cent more efficiently than usual. The result should be a fine white salt, which you mix with wood ash and sprinkle lightly on the newly turned earth, after ploughing but before the harrow. So go ahead, report me, I don't care. But I don't think your superiors are going to be all that interested."

～

I'd made a fool of myself, and I was ashamed of that. I'd forgotten the first rule; the customer is always right. If he wanted to trap me in a bottle and boil me down into nothing, he was entitled to do just that. True, it'd be the end of me—that's why alchemy is such a terrible thing; it changes all the rules, reevaluates all values, breaks down the fundamental order that we stand for. Along with necromancy, it's the worst possible thing a human being can do, and I'm not entirely sure we understand it ourselves. I can't believe I just said that. But I suspect it's true. If someone changes the rules, who knows what the rules are?

But when I made my silly outburst I hadn't thought it through properly. If he destroyed me, what would he have achieved? Nothing, except deprive himself of his helper and slave, the only means by which he could access the power he'd signed his soul away for. Made no sense. He'd have the rest of his seventeen years, but that was all; no infinite power, nothing. He needed me. He wouldn't do anything to hurt me. Surely.

But then, what would I know about the workings of a mind like that?

We still don't know what became of our friend and colleague who fell into the hands of Fortunatus of Perimadeia. We carry on searching for him but with little hope. As far as we are able to ascertain, he's fallen into a place beyond anything that we created or that we control—beyond good and evil, to coin a phrase—and the only man who could possibly tell us how to get there would have been Fortunatus of Perimadeia, who died centuries ago. Anyway, that's why even the thought of alchemy makes me shudder. It's a wicked, wicked thing to do.

As you can imagine, I kept a very sharp eye on him after that.

But to little avail. Think about it. How can you tell if a man's succeeded in turning base metal into gold in a place where there's gold everywhere you look? Literally. We were running short of storage space. All the dungeons and cellars were full; all the cupboards and wardrobes, every last toolshed and outhouse, anything you could put a padlock and hasp on, was bursting with ingots or earthenware pots of dust. Precisely because the supply was so plentiful and so easy to extract, the miners didn't seem inclined to retire or quit. No, they carried on producing, while the going was good, before the dream ended and they woke up. They couldn't be bothered or spare the time to cart their gold to the frontiers and sell it (and besides, they might get robbed on the way and lose it all). In any case, what were they going to sell it for? Food and drink were provided free of charge, likewise clothing and tools. This wasn't one of those gold rushes where the only people who really get rich are the sutlers and the boardinghouse keepers.

In such an environment, trying to keep track of the appearances and disappearances of small quantities of gold, as might be produced by alchemical processes, was out of the question. I tried standing behind him and watching every move he made very carefully, but he protested (quite reasonably) that I was getting in his way and ruining his concentration, and if I insisted on looming about like an architectural feature, would I please do it somewhere else? He was, it goes without saying, entirely within his rights to throw me out while he was working. As for making good my idiotic threat to report him—well. A sinner suspected of conspiring to commit sin. The only official response I could expect to that would be *So I should bloody well hope.*

～

My first experiment was entirely successful. I turned a mountain into gold.

At least, that was what I told him. Go and look for yourself, I said, pointing to an unremarkable hillock on the skyline. Take a spade, chip away the turf, and look beneath the surface. It'll be gold. Me, I'm so confident I can't be bothered to look, but feel free.

He gazed at me with that horrified, stupid look that people tend to wear when you start talking about alchemy. "You haven't," he said.

"I have."

"But that's—"

"Yes."

He hesitated, just for a moment; then there was a blur, he was gone, he was back again. "Why?" he said.

"Excuse me?"

"Why?" he repeated. "There's already more gold in these mountains than anyone could possibly hope to use. If you want gold, I'm duty bound to give it to you, in unlimited quantities. So, I repeat. Why?"

I shrugged. "To see if I could, I guess."

"Not good enough."

I laughed. "I forgot," I said, "you've got this bee in your bonnet about alchemy."

"You could put it that way."

"Though I really don't see why. I mean, what harm does it do anyone?"

"You know perfectly—"

"I admit," I said, "a grossly expanded gold supply could lead to inflation and devaluation of currencies, which might trigger an economic crisis. Though if you took the trouble to read my *Wealth of Nations,* you'd discover that an ample money supply can also fuel economic growth, particularly in circumstances of restricted credit. That's not what's upsetting you, is it?"

"I did read it," he said. "It's very good."

"You're afraid I'm going to stuff you in a bottle and kill you."

He looked at me. "You wouldn't do that."

"No, of course not. I value you too much. You're my friend."

A look of panic swept across his face. "No, I—"

"Yes," I said firmly. "You are. Yes, I know that the day will come when the bond will fall due and you'll lead me off to eternal torment. I accept that. All friends betray you, in the end. But until that day comes—" I shrugged. "We're friends. I wouldn't hurt you."

He sat down on an upturned barrel. Luckily he didn't weigh anything. "I'm not handling this very well," he said.

"Nobody's perfect."

That made him laugh. "I'm finding this assignment difficult," he said. "I'm sorry."

"Don't be. You're doing your best." I poured a glass of wine. He could smell it, at any rate. "I understand," I said. "You're a fundamentally decent person who happens to work for an employer whose values you don't always share. You aren't the first and I don't suppose you'll be the last. Don't have a crisis of conscience about it."

He lifted his head and looked at me. "Right now," he said, "I work for you."

"That's what I said," I reply. "You don't hold with alchemy, but never mind. If it's anybody's fault, it's mine. I accept full responsibility."

"You can't—"

I waited to learn what I couldn't do, but he'd shut up like a clam. I didn't press the issue. "Who knows," I said, "I might turn this whole country to gold. Isn't there a legend about that?"

He shuddered. "Please don't."

"Are you asking me as a friend?"

Alchemy indeed; to turn one thing into another—its opposite, its antithesis. Rock to gold, base to noble, enemy to friend. Indeed, it is unnatural, and I can see why it worried him so much. A reevaluation of all values; that's a quotation, isn't it? Oh yes. From me. Well.

To turn good into evil, right into wrong; and vice versa, of course. I was beginning to wish I'd stuck at alchemy when I was younger. Except back then I was fooling people, a fraud, a con man. At least I think I was. But then, I never did discover how that experiment came out.

Evil into good—take a demon, trap him in a flask, boil him up, and turn him into an angel. You can see why they'd be worried about that. Very worried indeed.

The barrel he'd sat on contained a new invention of mine, of which I was quite proud. I named it aqua tollens—to myself; naturally I couldn't tell anyone about it. For the record, it's a subtle blend of strong acids—vitriol and nitre—and sugar (no, it isn't; but I'm damned, excuse the expression, if I'm going to tell you what's in it or how to make it; I don't know you and I certainly wouldn't trust you with that stuff). It's so tricksy you have to mix the ingredients on a block of ice; and if a single drop of it falls a man's height onto the ground, it blasts a hole about as wide and deep as a good workman can dig in an hour. An invaluable aid, you'll agree, to the mining industry.

~

"I'd like you to do something for me," I told him. "But I'm afraid you won't want to."

Ever since we'd had our brief chat about alchemy he'd been different; wary, nervous, unsettled. "Your wish is my command," he said. "You know that."

"That's all very well," I said. "But I've given you a lot of anxiety and stress over this alchemy thing. I don't know. I'd better think about it some more."

"Please," he said wretchedly. "My feelings don't enter into it. Tell me what you want me to do."

"Well," I said. "I'd quite like you to raise the dead."

His eyes rolled, but he didn't say a word.

"It's just," I went on, "I'd quite like to see my wife again."

"The one you may or may not have murdered."

"I've only been married once," I said, a little frostily. "And I always tell people I murdered her, but really it was all her fault." I sighed. "We parted on bad terms, obviously. And it's been on my mind. I don't like to think she actually believes I killed her on purpose."

He'd turned a sort of pale grey, like a dove's stomach feathers. "First alchemy, then necromancy," he said. "You realise—"

"The two worst things a human being can do, yes, thank you. Though personally, I would interpret them as making some money and talking to my wife. Believe it or not, people do that sort of stuff every day and nobody gets particularly worked up about it."

The look in his eyes was more reproach than anything else. "You twist everything," he said.

"Guilty," I said. "Though I prefer to think of it as a form of art."

~

Which I couldn't really deny. Creativity—the ability to make something out of nothing; no, because we can do that, proverbially. The ability to take something and turn it into something else; that's more like it. The thing humans can do and we can't. Art. Alchemy. Fiction. Lies.

Raising the dead, however, is something quite other. There's nothing artistic about that. It's just wanton rule-breaking, pure and simple.

So I looked him in the eye and said, "When do you want to do this incredibly stupid, ill-advised thing?"

"How about right now?"

I shook my head. "It takes time," I said. "There are procedures, protocols, that sort of thing. You'll have to give me at least a week."

He laughed. "Don't be silly," he said. "You exist outside time and space."

He was starting to annoy me. "Quite. Even so. I'll need a week."

"Not if we do it my way."

I was so stunned I couldn't speak. If I needed to breathe, I'd have choked. "Your way—"

He nodded. "Maybe I've been a bit economical with the truth," he said. "The fact is, I want to talk to my wife."

"She's dead."

"Well." He pursed his lips. "Maybe, maybe not."

I very nearly lost my temper. "She's dead. You killed her."

"Sit down," he said. I interpreted that as an order. "She died from drinking an alchemical potion."

"Yes. One that you—"

"Quite. Let's not harp on too much about that." He sat down opposite me. "She thought I'd managed to concoct the serum of perpetual youth." He smiled sadly. "She was always a bit obsessive about staying young and beautiful. I think that's why she married me, because she thought I could do this elixir of life thing. Can't think of any other possible reason." He fell silent for a moment, then went on; "She was convinced I'd succeeded and was holding out on her. In fact what I was working on was your basic dross-into-gold process. She gobbled down half a pint of cinnabar and aqua regia, among other things. I'd told her it was poison. She didn't believe me."

I frowned at him. "That's all in your file."

"Indeed, I'm sure it is. But here's the thing." He hesitated, I don't know why. As though he were summoning up his courage. "The work I've been doing recently is basically perfecting those early experiments. I didn't know it at the time, but I was almost there; I'd cracked it, the great mystery, dross into gold. There were just one or two errors that needed to be ironed out and fixed; mostly to do with the imperfect sublimation of cinnabar." He looked at me and laughed. "Would you please not pull those dreadful faces," he said. "I know this is all stuff you don't like talking about, but you're going to have to bear with me if you want to understand what I'm trying to tell you. I think that the reason why the earlier version of the elixir didn't work—the one she drank—is because of a slight imbalance in the cinnabar's sublimation ratio. From what I've found out since and know now, I overcooked it a bit, which means it wasn't quite receptive enough to act on inorganic matter. Rock and metal and wood," he translated, unnecessarily. "But organic matter; flesh and blood—"

The implications hit me like a tidal wave. "A higher inclusion rate."

"Exactly." His eyes were shining. "You see, you know

all about it. Yes, the inclusion rate. It wouldn't work on base metal. But it would have an effect on flesh and blood." He looked straight at me. "I think what she drank really was the elixir of youth. Purely by accident, but it *was*."

"But she died."

"Did she? Or did she just lapse into a very deep coma while the sublimation took effect? It would look exactly like death to the naked eye. The flesh would be stone cold, the breathing so shallow it wouldn't mist a glass. Two weeks? Three? Like a butterfly in a chrysalis. Bear in mind, her lunatic brother had her body put into a bath of honey, to preserve it. Sick idea, really, but he was like that. The point is, we wouldn't have noticed the lack of decomposition. And then," he went on, "I blew up the palace and left in a hurry. So I have no idea what happened after that."

"The body would've been destroyed in the blast."

He shook his head. "Flesh sublimated by cinnabar? No power on Earth could even scratch it. If I'm right, she's not dead at all. She's still out there, and not a day over twenty-eight."

My mind was reeling. "So what do you want me to do?"

"Easy," he said, quite calmly. "I want you to find her."

~

27,886 women called Eudoxia living in the Northern hemisphere and aged between 24 and 34. None of them was her. 1,338,765 women of the right age living in the Northern hemisphere and answering her description. The one we were looking for was the 1,337,816th. So it goes.

Her name was Heloria, and she was married to a respectable salt merchant in eastern Blemya. She wasn't from those parts; that was obvious. How she came to be there she had no idea. Her earliest memory was waking up in the ruined shell of a collapsed building, with a roofbeam trapping her ankle. A party of looters, scrounging for floor tiles, found her and pulled her out; she went with them, having nowhere else to go, but they got sick of her temper and constant complaining and turned her out into the street. Her memory might have been a blank but she realised the danger she was in. Fortuitously she walked past the door of the Cold Star convent. The sisters were very kind to her, and she stayed there for a long time—six months, something like that—hoping her memory would come back. When it didn't, she had to make a choice. Did she want to stay with the sisters and devote her life to contemplation and prayer? No, she realised, not in the slightest. She could read and write and do arithmetic. The sisters found her a place as a book-keeper with a patron of their order, a good man who could be trusted not to take advantage of a vulnerable young woman. Three months after that they were married, and she'd been perfectly happy ever since.

I showed him a vision of her. "Yes," he said, "that's my Eudoxia. I'd know her anywhere."

I was reading the file. "It can't be her," I said. "Listen. She turned up on the sisters' doorstep seven years ago. She's been married to the salt merchant for six years. You blew up Prince Phocas forty-one years ago. The figures don't tally."

He frowned. "It looks just like her," he said. "I could've sworn it was her." He thought for a moment. "When was Phocas's palace rebuilt?"

Back to the files. "It wasn't," I said.

"It must have been. Prime real estate in the middle of the city."

I shook my head. "Because of the way it was destroyed," I told him. "Nobody wanted to go anywhere near the place, they reckoned it was bewitched. The only people who went there were thieves and looters."

He turned and looked at me.

"It's possible," I said slowly. "She could have been there all that time. Could she?" I added.

"Why are you asking me?"

"Well, you're the expert," I said irritably. "You know about alchemy, probably more than we do. As I've been trying to get you to understand, it's a subject we really don't choose to dwell on."

He was silent for a long time. "It's possible," he said. "After all, nobody has ever done that experiment before, so it's anybody's guess how long the transmutation process takes. It could've been thirty-odd years, I just don't know. Or maybe, once the process is complete, you hibernate like a caterpillar in a cocoon until somebody wakes you up." He shook his head like a wet dog. "This is silly," he said. "Why are we speculating, when you've got all the facts at your fingertips? Of course you know who she is; name, date and place of birth, date and place of death, come to that. You know everything."

I looked away, deeply ashamed. He was asking me for something—as was his right under the contract—and I couldn't give it to him.

Yes, we're omniscient. Of course we are. And to us, all things are possible.

Up to a point.

Take human beings, for instance. We can track and trace any human being in an instant. Except that there are exceptions. Tiny ones, of indescribable rarity. Exceptions so trivial and insignificant that they can't conceivably matter. And they aren't really exceptions at all, because they're all to do with that single unbearable overriding abomination, alchemy.

A human being who's been alchemically altered ceases, as far as our tracking and tracing protocols are concerned, to exist. Logical; the natural thing that stems from the Created has gone, having been unnaturally altered into something else. The something else, being beyond and outside nature, exists in spite of us—we don't recognise it, the way a government doesn't recognise the bunch of pirates and thieves who've seized power in the kingdom next door.

This woman, the one Saloninus claimed as his Eudoxia, bore no trace. She wasn't in the records. As far as we were concerned, before the moment she woke up in the ruins of Phocas's palace, she hadn't existed.

Oh dear cubed and recubed.

~

This was too much. I consulted my superiors.

It only took an instant, and I'm sure Saloninus didn't even notice I'd gone. I travelled to the office of the Supreme Archive. As luck would have it, the deputy chief is an old acquaintance of mine.

"It's possible," he said.

He seemed curiously guarded, which I put down to the disgust and horror that alchemy stirs in all of us. "I know it's possible," I said. "What I need to know is, can there be any other explanation?"

He was quiet for a moment. "This wretched woman doesn't show up anywhere," he said. "Right until the moment she wakes up with the beam across her." He pulled down a ledger from a shelf. "The princess Eudoxia similarly disappears from the record at the moment when she drank the potion. I invite you to draw your own conclusions."

"Done that," I snapped. "What I want—sorry, what I desperately need—is an alternative version. Anything. Anything I can sincerely believe in. Otherwise, you don't need me to tell you, we're in real trouble."

He looked at me, and I could see what he was thinking; no, *you're* in trouble, not me, thank goodness. I was annoyed by that. For pity's sake, we're all on the same side, the same team. Why can't people accept that and work together? Still, there you go. "The only other explanation," he said, "is that our system of archives and information storage and retrieval is so hopelessly inefficient and shot through with so many systemic faults and errors that in a case like this—irregular, as it were, not complying with normal practice in several key areas—a human could simply slip through the net, so to speak. But that," he added sternly, "is impossible."

"Is it? I'm asking you as a friend. Be honest with me."

"Absolutely," replied the deputy chief archivist. "It could never happen."

~

Next I went to see my supervisor. "I can spare you five minutes," he said. His idea of a joke.

"It's alchemy," I told him. "It has to be."

"It does look that way," he replied. "Unfortunate."

I was amazed at how calmly he seemed to be taking it. "Saloninus has found a method of performing alchemical transmutation that actually works," I told him. "That's a disaster, surely."

He pursed his lips. "It's very bad," he said. "Given the contractual relationship."

That struck me as an odd thing to say. "It changes everything, surely."

He chose to interpret that as a play on words, which I hadn't intended it to be, and gave me a thin smile. "Not quite everything," he said. "It's not like it's the first time it's happened."

News to me. "You mean, there have been others?"

"Oh yes." He nodded solemnly. "None of which ever came to anything. The outbreak was always contained, if you want to look at it in those terms. The contagion never spread. The alchemist always died very soon after making his discovery, and his secret always died with him. Usually," he added, "there was an explosion. Dreadfully unstable materials these people use. A terrific explosion, and all the notes and equipments destroyed in the blast."

I wasn't entirely sure I liked the sound of that. "You make it sound like the explosions weren't accidents."

He frowned at me. "Alchemy is an abomination," he said. "It's not natural. Unnatural things can't exist in nature, they're intrinsically unstable. That's why the materials alchemists use are so exceptionally volatile. It's in their nature to blow up."

I decided I didn't want to think about the implications of that. "Saloninus succeeded," I said. "And survived."

"Well, he's a special case, isn't he?" my supervisor snapped. "Extraordinary man. He sets up the ultimate experiment and then walks away before it's complete. He sets it up precisely because he *knows* it's liable to explode—taking all his enemies with it, yes, but to start the procedure and not to care about the result; it's unthinkable, literally. He had the answer to the secret of the universe in his hands, but he was more interested in saving his own neck and making money. Extraordinary man."

"He is."

"Yes. And that's not a good thing. You do realise," he went on, "that the contract means that if he's conducting alchemical research, even if he blows himself up, he won't die. It won't stop him. We've guaranteed that he can't die in war or by accident." Suddenly he laughed, not in a healthy way. "You have to hand it to him," he said. "The contract, selling his soul to us, is the only way he could be sure of conducting his research and living to tell the tale."

My head was starting to spin. "If he's made this woman immortal," I said, "what's to prevent him doing the same thing to himself?"

My supervisor looked at me. "What indeed?" he said. "Nothing, is the answer to that. And if he's immortal, he won't ever die. Bear in mind, the second part of the contract between him and us only comes into effect at the moment of his death. If he never dies—"

I shook my head. "The contract's for twenty years."

"Wrong," my supervisor said grimly. "We guarantee him twenty years. At the end of that period, we withdraw our support, the action of his natural functions is resumed, and he dies. But if his natural functions have been superseded by some appalling chemical and he doesn't die—" He held up both hands. "It's you I feel sorry for."

"Me?"

"Oh yes. Bear in mind, under the contract you're

bound to be his servant for life."

Believe it or not, I'd been so preoccupied with the cosmic implications of the situation that I hadn't stopped to consider what it could mean for me personally. Not that that could possibly matter; I live to serve, my existence is founded and centred on my function as a willing tool. Even so.

"There's got to be something we can do," I said.

He gave me a sad smile. "Indeed," he said. "And I'm open to suggestions."

~

The thing about me that seems to puzzle people the most—people who know me, who believe what I tell them—is that I can write the most profound things without actually meaning them. I can persuade people of things I don't myself believe, or (more usually) simply don't care about.

Take, for example, my greatest philosophical works, in which I demonstrate the vacuity and inanity of superstition and belief in the supernatural, demolish all existing moral and ethical systems and reveal the truth about Man, that he's an animal that needs to delude himself in order to live. Man, I argue accordingly, is therefore something to be overcome, evolved beyond, left behind. Only by evolving ourselves into the higher human being, the superman—

But you know all that. You've read it, or a potted summary. If you aren't convinced by it, it's only because you haven't taken the trouble to read it properly and follow the arguments.

Do I believe any of that? I don't know, I've never given it much thought. I wrote that particular sequence of tracts for a particular patron, a man who loathed the priesthood and didn't like being taken to task for breaking various laws. He paid well, and I needed the money.

I started from the premise, which sort of came with the brief, that priests and religion are full of shit; from there it followed naturally that the morality they espouse must be false or faulty. Having established the side I was on, I looked around for arguments to support it. I found they came quite easily to me. I started with various inconsistencies in religious doctrine, and found that they derived from compromises made by long-ago ecumenical councils to reconcile violent political disputes within the clerical hierarchy. I argued, if the priests make up bits of doctrine to suit themselves, maybe they made up the whole thing. From there it was no big deal to demonstrate that they'd done exactly that. The Book as we know it proved to be not a monolithic and unambiguous record of the word of the Invincible Sun, but rather a negotiated construct, patched together from four or five sources, revised and edited and redacted by generations of scholars, some of whom belonged to such and such a sect or interest group, others of whom supported diametrically opposite positions or interests. It was no bother at all to show that the Book was a political object with no real credibility. And once you've knocked out the Book, you've dealt religion a blow from which it can never recover.

Of course I had my doubts. I could see that it was entirely possible that the Invincible Sun had indeed spoken to His prophets—once, long ago—and ever since, the prophets and their successors had spent all their time and energy misreporting, misrepresenting, and generally screwing around with what He had told them. That was a valid interpretation, and if I'd chosen to espouse it, I bet you I could have made it every bit as convincing as the argument I put my whole weight behind, namely the case for the prosecution. But nobody was going to pay me to do that, so I didn't.

From that foundation, everything else sort of followed organically. My patron was thrilled with what I'd done for him, and gave me a great deal of money to write some more. Did I believe any of it? I don't know. I preferred to keep an open mind. Just as a good general puts himself into the mind of his opponent—if I were him, what would I do in this situation?—I inhabited both sides of the argument, a kind of double agent looking to betray everybody. The fact is, the more you look for something, the likelier you are to find it, even if it isn't actually there; sooner or later, if you look hard enough, you'll find *something*. The trick is then to interpret what you've found as what you were looking for.

So; it was all for money. Let's consider money, shall we, just for a moment.

When I was a kid, we had it. My father was, to all appearances, a wealthy gentleman farmer. I grew up not thinking about money the way fish don't think about water. Then, while I was away at the Studium, my father died and it turned out there was no money after all. The water had all vanished, and I was the fish on dry land, twisting in agony, unable to breathe.

I was twenty years old; no skill, no trade. I suppose I should've touted round for work as a clerk—I could read and write, and people pay you a living wage for doing both, but I was spoilt, I couldn't possibly live on a living wage, I'd suffocate. I considered, therefore, the ways in which I could obtain money, given the resources I had and those I lacked. They were:

Literary, artistic, and scientific excellence.

Deception.

Theft.

Arguments for and against all of these. The first one is the safest, but it takes too long, is uncertain and insecure, and doesn't pay enough. The second is safer than the third, but usually takes a bit of setting-up; not much use when you haven't eaten for three days and the soles of your shoes have just fallen off. The third is risky, downright terrifying, but answers the immediate, pressing need. Luckily, I was good at all three.

I made money; making it and holding on to it are two different things. I could never quite earn or steal enough; the one big score always eluded me. I trimmed back my expectations to the bone and found I was perfectly content with the austere life of the scholar—plain but regular meals, a roof over my head, that was fine by me. Unfortunately, every time I got my hands on secure tenure and settled down, some past indiscretion from my thieving and deceiving days would come swooping back to haunt me and drive me back on the road. I spent an awful lot of time sleeping in ditches and derelict barns, and all because I'd been afraid of having to do without the comforts of affluence. My big deceptions, such as the alchemy scam I pulled on my college friend Prince Phocas, tended to blow up (often literally) in my face. More and more of my intelligence and ingenuity was getting used up on digging myself out of the trouble I'd got myself into. The spade I used for this digging was, as often as not, my knack for philosophy, poetry, and science; they paid the bills and induced patrons to shield me from my enemies, so I developed them, the way you build up certain muscles by constant use. The stuff I came up with no longer interested me in the least, beyond what someone was prepared to give me for it. Simple as that. Do bees necessarily like honey? I don't know. Who cares?

When the one big score finally came along—the recipe for synthetic blue paint—I reckoned that all my troubles were finally over and I could at last relax, calm down, and be myself. I could do the important work I knew I was capable of, or simply lie in the sun and eat raisins, or both. And then it suddenly struck me; I was sixty-seven years old, and most people don't live much past seventy. I'd got back to where I started from, but it was too late.

It was time, I told myself, to start considering my options.

The great thing about not necessarily believing in your beliefs is that it's so much easier to revise them. What, I asked myself, if I'd been all wrong about religion, the supernatural, magic, and the Divine? What if it really exists? I set out to prove that it did; and (having the incentive, just as I'd had the incentive to prove the opposite years ago) I succeeded. Having established that, I was in a position to address the real issue. How could I persuade, bluff, charm, or trick the Divine into giving me what I wanted?

~

They stared at me. Eventually, one of them said, "That's unheard of."

I wasn't going to be put off by mere staring. "Nevertheless," I said.

But one of them shook his head. "You're going to have to do better than that," he said.

On the way out, I reflected on the way in which so many mortals pray. It's strictly a rational proposition. If He exists, they argue, it's best to be on the right side of Him; if He doesn't, well, no harm done, it hasn't cost anything. I'm not like that, unfortunately. Either I believe or I don't. And I believed—thought I believed—in the doctrines of Saloninus concerning the invalidity of conventional morality. I believed that there are no absolutes of good and evil and that all that matters, in the final analysis, is which side you're on. It was, I felt, a doctrine which accorded exactly with my own observations and experience.

The problems start when your side isn't on your side anymore.

I had one more call to pay.

We're supposed to observe the chain of command, but it's not an absolute requirement. It's recognised that there are times when you have to bypass all that and go straight to the top. This, I felt certain, was one of them.

Not the *top* top, of course. The highest I could aspire to was Divisional Command. It meant a great deal of heel-kicking in anterooms, but time where we come from isn't exactly linear. Still, I should've taken a book to read while I was hanging about.

I was shown in, and explained the situation as concisely as I could. "So you see," I concluded, "we definitely have a problem."

"You think so."

The thing about Divisional Command is, they seem to have this antipathy to answering questions.

"Yes, I do," I said. "Here's a mortal who appears to have perfected the process of alchemical transmutation. Normally, the very act of doing so would result in his immediate death, by explosion, since the compounds that effect the change are inherently unstable. That's why we're not knee-deep in immortal humans. But this one is smart. If he blows himself up, by the terms of this wretched contract, we have to protect him. He's outsmarted us. He's won."

"You think so?"

"I do." I paused, trying to interpret the blank, hollow

stare facing me. "If he succeeds in performing the transmutation, naturally he won't keep quiet about it. Or even if he tries to, word will get out. People will know that alchemy works, that it's possible to achieve eternal life. Millions will blow themselves up trying to do it. A few will succeed."

"You think so."

"Yes, just look at this Eudoxia woman. She drank the stuff. There was the usual explosion, but she survived. She hasn't aged a day in forty years. Without knowing precisely what he did, I can't tell you the extent to which the process is reproducible, but it makes me feel sure that it can work, sometimes. What with that, and the wholescale carnage of those who try and fail, I think you'll agree, it's an impossible situation. We have to do something."

"What do you have in mind?"

I felt the whole weight of Creation on my shoulders. "We have two options," I said. "One of them is to break our word. We find some way of stopping him, even though it means lying, misleading, or downright force."

"What do you have in mind?"

I closed my eyes. This was all really hard for me. "What happens to us," I asked, "if we breach the contract? For example, what would be the consequences if we killed him? His mortal body, I mean. For sure, it would mean the deal is off; we wouldn't get his immortal soul for perpetual torment. I for one could live with that. But would we have to restore his body to life, wind the clock back so that the killing never took place? Can we actually do that, because strictly speaking it'd be necromancy, which is forbidden? Of course, so is murder."

"What do you think?"

"I think we're in so much trouble that anything we do is going to have bad repercussions. Being seen to have broken our word will mean that mortals will no longer trust us. We can forget about future contracts of this sort. Again, I can live with that."

"Is that all?"

I shook my head. "I don't know who enforces our rules against us," I said. "We do, presumably. If he has a valid complaint against us, who does he appeal to? Who judges us? What can they do to us, if they find against us?"

"What do you think?"

"I think I don't want to find out," I said firmly. "I think that going down that road is unthinkable. We *do not* break our word. We *do not* assassinate those who pose us problems. The pursuit of expediency is a luxury we don't have."

"Why?"

"Because it would force us to answer the question I

just asked," I said. "I guess."

"What's the other option you talked about?"

I sighed. "Simple," I said. "We buy him off."

～

A split second later, I was back. As I'd hoped, Saloninus hadn't noticed I'd been gone.

"It's her, then," I said.

"I think it could well be," he replied.

We were standing behind an invisible wall, watching her; we could see her, she couldn't see us. She was combing her hair, getting ready for another day of doing whatever it is that mortal women do. I'm no judge of these things, but she seemed perfectly happy.

"Thank you," Saloninus said.

"Excuse me? What for?"

"For setting my mind at rest," he said. "All these years I've been torn up with guilt about what I did to her. Well, you know that. I always say I murdered her, even though I knew it was an accident. Now it turns out she's not dead. In fact, she got exactly what she wanted: eternal youth and beauty. I feel so much better now. Thank you."

"Don't mention it," I said.

He breathed out long and slow, then turned to me. "We've intruded on her privacy long enough, don't you think? Let's go."

I was confused. "Don't you want her back? I thought—"

He grinned. "Dear me, no. I never liked her much. Dreadful woman. But she didn't deserve to die like that. But she didn't, so everything's fine. And she seems so much happier than she ever did when I used to know her, and she was a princess. Come on, I want to go home now."

Back at the shack, I sat down on the barrel of explosive. "What's this for?" I asked.

"That? I told you. It's for blasting the deeper seams."

"It'll be years before anyone gets that far down," I said. "What's it really for?"

He smiled at me. "There's no kidding you, is there? It's for a little experiment I mean to try."

I waited, then said, "What?"

"I'm going to blow myself up."

I was looking straight at him. As far as I know, my face didn't move at all. I have infinitely better control over my face than any human. "Why?"

"To see if my research has been successful. If it has, being blown up won't hurt me. If not—" He grinned. "I may need your help, in that case. Under the terms of the contract."

I did some calculations. Based on what he'd told me

earlier, the contents of the barrel would dig a crater large enough to hold the island of Scona. "The whole barrel?"

He shrugged. "In my opinion, bangs can never be too loud."

"When are you planning on doing this?"

"When I'm ready. No point in rushing things. I've got seventeen years, after all."

I stood up. "The gold," I said. "It's not just for politics, is it?"

"Maybe not."

"To make the elixir of life, you need gold. It's a key ingredient. You're planning on making a huge batch of the stuff. And then you're going to give it to as many people as possible."

He gazed at me, and I couldn't read his face. "Now why would I want to do a thing like that?"

~

To raise an army of immortals. To storm Heaven.

Well, it'd be an option. I believe in options. I think everybody should have as many of them as possible.

Could it be done? I really don't know. Of course, you'd have to persuade them to try. How would you sell an idea like that to a bunch of thieves, outlaws, mercenaries, and professional desperados? You'd need a certain degree of eloquence, a way with words. Come to think of it, I've got that.

Maybe not actually storming Heaven, at least not to begin with. Start with a modest, attainable goal and work upward from there. First, conquer the world; an immortal army could do that standing on its head. Defy the gods; set yourself up in their place. I give you the superman; man is something to be evolved up from. What is the defining limitation of Man? His mortality. Take away that, and his pathetic need for his daily bread, and his health and physical safety—now he's equal with the gods on that score, their superior in so much more; all the arts and sciences he's learned in the days of his mortality make him stronger than the gods, now that he's escaped the great restriction. Consider men and elephants; consider which one hunts, kills, tames the other. Man is small but clever; the elephant is big but stupid. Being small made us need to be clever. We're smarter than the gods. Need proof? Look at me. Living proof; the emphasis being on the living.

He was right about the crucial role of gold in alchemy; he got there, eventually. Not soon enough to beat me to it; he arrived at the realisation just nicely in time to save me the effort of explaining it to him.

In the course of my travels, I've seen the most extraordinary things. For example: in the Blemyan desert there are sandstone cliffs, split by earthquakes. In those rifts you can find the bones of giant monstrous creatures, buried long ago. Now, you don't have to be a genius to figure out that once upon a time, that desert was actually the bottom of the sea. The sandstone cliffs were once the seabed, and the bones are the remains of huge sea-creatures, who died, drifted to the bottom, and sank into the soft mud, a hundred feet deep. Clearly a lot of time has passed since then—thousands of years, maybe, who knows? The bones themselves have rotted away, and what you're actually seeing is an impression in the sand, squashed into rock by the sheer weight of the water. They were remarkable animals, those sea-monsters; forty, sixty, a hundred feet long, enormously strong, unbelievably powerful. But look at their tiny little heads, and then discount the space inside those heads taken up with bone, muscle, sinew, eyes, ears, and other ancillary equipment. Those awesomely strong monarchs of the deep had brains the size of walnuts. And so it is, as far as I can tell, with the gods. All power and no intellect. Strength makes you stupid. It's the weak who grow smart.

And what makes us weak? The passage of time. That's all.

Man is something to be out-evolved.

~

You're not supposed to be always on the doorstep clamouring for instructions. Use your discretion and your initiative, they say, that's why you're the grade you are. And then, when it all goes wrong, it's all your fault. What on Earth possessed you to do all that without checking back first? How could you have been so stupid?

So back I went. You can never tell, of course, but I had the distinct impression he'd been expecting me.

"It gets worse," I told him. "He's brewing up gallons of the stuff. Enough for an army."

"Is that right?"

"That's not all. He's also invented a super-weapon."

He gazed at me, as though I were the view from a high window. "What sort of weapon?"

"An explosive," I said. "An eggcupful blasts a hole big enough to bury a man in."

That provoked a frown from the impassive face. "Is that right?"

"I did a full analysis," I said. "It's just nitre and vitriol mixed with distilled honey. You don't need me to tell you what that means."

"Tell me anyway."

"It means the ingredients are in plentiful supply. He

could cook up thousands of gallons of the stuff. Millions. He could brew up enough to blow up the world."

Silence. Then: "Why would anyone want to do that?"

Such an odd question to ask. "It's a threat," he said. "Think about it. He has an immortal army, and a weapon that can destroy the Earth."

"Do you seriously believe he could overcome us?"

I shook my head. "That's not how mortals think. I think he's going to issue an ultimatum; hand over power, or I'll destroy everything. It's death," I explained. "It colours every aspect of how mortal minds work. Everything is conceived of in finite terms. If I've got to go, I'll take the whole lot with me."

Another silence. "Do you think he'd be capable of that?"

"He's Saloninus. He's capable of anything."

He looked at me again. This time, I was some sort of optical illusion, something that couldn't possibly exist, but did. "Do you think he wants to rule Heaven and Earth?"

Now that was a question I hadn't asked myself. But I found the answer came to me without much hesitation. "I think he feels he has no choice. It's that or eternal damnation. Again, it's how mortals do things. Think of palace coups; a man kills the king and takes his throne because if he doesn't he knows he'll be executed. They're such an all-or-nothing species."

"If he were to blow up the world, wouldn't we simply rebuild it?"

My turn to be silent for a moment. "Would we, though? Or would we wash our hands of the whole experiment and move on to something else?"

"Would we?"

I shrugged. On a need-to-know basis, presumably. "I can't possibly make decisions when the stakes are as high as this. I need instructions. What should I do?"

He turned his face away. "Need you ask?"

~

Well; since my superiors in my organisation had failed me, I turned for guidance to a source of wisdom I had always believed in and trusted. Fortunately, I had a copy with me. Signed by the author.

I opened the book at random. I saw—

I give you the superman. Man is something to be overcome.

Indeed. Make some immortal, blow up the rest. Evolution takes no prisoners. A loathsome philosophy, but hard to argue against. Repulsive, but entirely valid. Otherwise, the Earth would still be populated by giant pea-brained lizards.

(Actually, I remember them with affection; even though they spent their entire lives poised between blood-lust and mortal terror, eating and being eaten, trampling down forests with every pace, and stealing each others' eggs from the nest, at least they never invented morality. Simpler times. Happier times.)

There's a sect somewhere who believe that in the beginning, humans lived in a beautiful garden, completely unaware of right and wrong, good and evil. Then a wicked snake tricked them into learning about it—ethics, morality—and everything went downhill from there. I rather like that story.

Could I stand idly by and see the world blown up, Mankind exterminated, replaced in the gear-train of evolution by the immortal, warlike superman, a subtle blend of artists, whores, and highway robbers? There was a sort of wonderful logic to it. Take anything to its logical conclusion and you're likely to end up with the grotesque and the absurd.

I realised I knew the answer. Man is not something to be overcome. Man is something to be kept firmly in its place.

~

K. J. Parker

"I know what you're up to," I said.

He was sitting at his desk in that ghastly shack, looking at the view. It was one of the good days. The mist had cleared and the sun was out, bathing the mountains in pale gold; you could almost believe that his men had been out there early, scraping off all the turf. The usual biting easterly wind had dropped, and from that angle you couldn't see the hideous scars of the open-cast mines. Too beautiful to be blown up, I decided. Worth saving.

He put down the book he'd been reading; Amphitryon of Scona on the properties of materials. "Do you really?"

"Yes. And you can't do it."

He frowned. "You're not supposed to tell me what I can and can't do. It's in the contract."

"Damn the contract."

He seemed to find that mildly amusing. "Go on, then," he said. "What am I up to?"

I took a deep breath. "You're going to raise an immortal army, besiege Heaven, and threaten to blow up the Earth." He didn't react. I went on; "It's useless, of course. You can't win."

"Neither can you."

Maybe some tiny part of me had still been hoping I'd been wrong. If so, it died. "Anything you destroy we can

116

rebuild. In the blink of an eye."

He nodded. "Yes," he said. "If you've a mind to."

I had nothing more to say, so I glared at him. He said, "There's a legend about how your lot got so fed up with the iniquities of the world that they sent a great flood. The idea was to kill off everything and start again. In fact, you changed your mind and killed off nearly everything. Of course, it's only a legend, though I find myself asking, was that the flood that trapped the giant lizards in the sandstone cliffs? Anyway, that's beside the point. Would you rebuild it, if I blew it up? You don't know. You can't be sure. And you love the world. You love the human race, and its art and its literature. Considerably more, I guess, than I do." He smiled at me. "And it's your call."

"Of course it's not," I said. (And I thought, so that's what lying feels like. Overrated.) "Do you really think they'd leave the future of your species in my hands? But I am authorised to offer you a deal."

Just for a split second—a split second in my timescale, so a very short time indeed—I thought I saw something in his eyes; the faintest reflection of a vast, unfathomable smugness. But it passed, and he said, "I don't want a deal. I've already got one, thank you very much. I've got a contract."

I nodded. "Of course," I said. "A contract which you know you can cheat on. A contract which depends on your death, which we both know will never happen, once you've drunk that horrible potion."

He raised one finger in tacit acknowledgement. I could've hit him.

"I know exactly what you've got in mind," I said. "Immortal armies, laying siege to Heaven, threatening to blow up the world unless we abdicate and go away." For a moment words failed me. "I thought better of you than that," I said.

He frowned, almost as though what I'd said had had some effect on him. Wishful thinking on my part, I'm sure. "I don't see that I have much choice," he said. "It's godhead or hellfire."

"Then you shouldn't have signed the contract in the first place."

He paused before replying. "My life passed me by so fast," he said. "And I realised, I'd spent it all lying and cheating, and nothing to show for it. All that talent, wasted. Really, the only person I'd cheated was myself. It was a gamble, sure. But I had nothing to lose. That's being mortal for you. I don't suppose you could possibly understand."

That hurt me a little. Maybe it's true, and I have spent too long among these people. Or not long enough. "There's an alternative," I said.

"I don't think so."

"Do you really want to blow up the world? Do you really want to kill millions of people?"

"Did your lot want to kill millions of people when they sent the great flood? Or millions of sea-monsters, or giant lizards, it doesn't really matter. Evolution has no compassion. Besides, they're all condemned to death anyway, so what difference does it make? But my supermen—"

"A handful."

"Only a few," he conceded. "We few, we happy few. Just think what I'm offering to my species. The next level." He smiled. "You said you liked my doctrine of sides. Well, I'm on their side, and you're on yours. Sorry. I wish we could've been friends."

"There's an alternative," I repeated.

He looked at me for a long time, during which the cock crowed thrice. "Go on, then," he said. "I'm listening."

$\sim$

From my sleeve I took the brass tube containing the contract. I held it out. "Yours," I said. "You can take it and put it in the fire. There will be no contract. Your soul will not be forfeit."

He didn't move, didn't even breathe, for ever so long.

"And in return?"

"All your alchemy equipment," I said, "and your notes and your chemicals go in a big heap down at the bottom of the valley. Then you roll your barrel of hellbrew off the cliff on top of it. And you never, ever even think about practising alchemy again."

He frowned. "If you're saying we put the clock back—"

"No." I shook my head. "You can keep the restored youth, and Mysia, all of that. You'll have fifty or sixty years of natural life, and then you'll go quietly and enjoy eternal bliss with the elect in paradise, or whatever."

He smiled. "Apart from that, we just forget all about it and pretend it never happened?"

"You make it sound shabby and something to be ashamed of. It's a good deal." I paused. "Please," I said. "I'm asking you as a friend."

He looked at me. "Oh, in that case," he said, and held out his hand.

～

I changed my mind about one thing. We didn't roll the barrel off the cliff. I didn't want anyone—especially the New Mysians, that collection of cutthroats and intellectuals—learning that it was possible for a human being to make any sort of weapon that powerful. Instead, we poured the stuff a trickle at a time down a deep, deep fissure into the very bowels of the Earth, into the broiling sea of molten magma. Then we dropped in the books, the notebooks, the stills, and the alembics.

He straightened up and looked at me. "It's all still in here." He tapped the side of his head. "Somewhere," he added.

I shuddered. "That's your guarantee," I said. "But just because you've got it doesn't mean you have to use it."

"Exactly." He beamed at me. He had a very charming smile. "Let's be civilised about it."

Then I gave him the brass tube. He fished out the sheet of parchment and showed it to me. "You never checked," he said.

"What?"

"Look." He pointed. At the foot of the page, where his signature should be, he'd written *Nemo Neminis filiu*: nobody son of no one. "I distracted you, remember? At the moment of signing. Invalid signature, invalid contract." Then he tore the paper into little bits, and ate them. "I imagine you could get into a lot of trouble for that," he said. "But the evidence is gone, so what the hell. It can be our secret."

I felt a cold hand brush my analogue for a heart. A lot of trouble, indeed. I hated him and loved him, all in the same moment.

"Thanks," I said.

"Don't mention it." He stepped back from the fissure. A waft of hot air rose up, enough to singe a mortal's hair. That would be the explosive, I guessed. "Well," he said, "it's been interesting. Any time you're passing, do drop in and take a look at the art."

"I'd like that," I heard myself say, and realised I meant it. "One thing," I said. "The artists. I know you wanted them for the perfect genetic mix, for your supermen—"

He shook his head. "That only occurred to me once they were here," he said. "They were for you. Because you like to look at paintings."

I felt a tightness in my throat. "I wish I could believe that."

He smiled. "Believe what you like," he said, and walked away.

$$\sim$$

Of course it was a gamble. And of course I got lucky.

The biggest stroke of luck—the thing that gave me the whole idea in the first place—was stumbling across the amnesiac woman. I don't know who the hell she was—obviously—but when her family called me in and asked if there was anything I could do for her, it suddenly came to me, fully formed and perfect, in a flash. I paid them a lot of money for her—despicable, a family who'd sell their own flesh and blood to a perfect stranger—and arranged for her to be found in the ruins of Phocas's palace. That was the luck.

The gamble was that their system of archives and records was quite as chaotic as I thought it must be, after years and years of diligent research. It was a huge risk, though I'd covered myself with the invalid signature—still, that silly little trick wasn't much to fall back on, in the event that I'd grossly miscalculated. But I hadn't; they really are as grossly inefficient in their record-keeping as I'd assumed, and of course the relevant officials would do everything they could to cover up their negligence; up to and including their gross exaggeration of the power of alchemy. That, of course, was what gave me the clue. I know for a fact alchemy doesn't work, but Heaven treats it as the worst possible sin. Why get so worked up about a nonexistent threat? Answer: someone somewhere is covering something up. Discrepancies in the records? Blame them on the alchemists. Once I'd reached that conclusion, all I had to do was figure out how to take advantage.

So; I did it. The one big score. I rule a kingdom literally built on top of a mountain of gold, from my throneroom in an impregnable castle. My subjects are the

TOR·COM

Science fiction. Fantasy. The universe.

And related subjects.

*

More than just a publisher's website, *Tor.com*
is a venue for **original fiction, comics,** and
discussion of the entire field of SF and fantasy,
in all media and from all sources. Visit our site
today — and join the conversation yourself.

CPSIA information can be obtained at www.ICGtesting.com
Printed in the USA
BVOW08s1732100316

439857BV00003B/40/P